NIPS
XI

D0513001

'A rare book — a great idea whose originality and quality is
carried through to the final mouthful of curry.'

Pam Macintyre, *The Australian's Review of Books*

'Like the best in children's literature, *NIPS XI* is a novel that
helps children explore their place in the world and
discover their own uniqueness ... *NIPS XI* simply bowled
me over ... funny and empowering ...'

Raymond Huber, *Viewpoint*

Takeaways

Are You Listening?, Lydia Sturton

Artists Are Crazy and Other Stories, Ken Catran

Blue Fin, Colin Thiele

The Changeling, Gail Merritt

Chickenpox, Yuck!, Josie Montano

The Dog King, Paul Collins

Dragon's Tear, Sue Lawson

Fake ID, Hazel Edwards

Fries, Ken Catran

Get a Life!, Krista Bell

The Grandfather Clock, Anthony Hill

The Great Ferret Race, Paul Collins

It's Time, Cassandra Klein, Karen R. Brooks

Jodie's Journey, Colin Thiele

The Keeper, Rosanne Hawke

Landslide, Colin Thiele

The Lyrebird's Tail, Susan Robinson

Mystery at Devon House, Cory Daniells

Monstered, Bernie Monagle

Ned's Kang-u-roo, Vashti Farrer

NewBjorn, Kathryn England

NIPS XI, Ruth Starke

NIPS Go National, Ruth Starke

No Regrets, Krista Bell

Pop Starlets, Josie Montano

Read My Mind!, Krista Bell

The Rescue of Princess Athena, Kathryn England

Sailmaker, Rosanne Hawke

Saving Saddler Street, Ruth Starke

The Sea Caves, Colin Thiele

Seashores and Shadows, Colin Thiele

Space Games, Mike Carter

Spy Babies, Ian Bone

Swan Song, Colin Thiele

Timmy, Colin Thiele

Twice upon a Time, John Pinkney

Wendy's Whale, Colin Thiele

Who Cares?, Krista Bell

The Worst Year of My Life, Katherine Goode

Ruth Starke

Lothian
BOOKS

ACKNOWLEDGEMENTS

I knew very little about cricket before I wrote this book, and I'm grateful to those who gave me help and encouragement. In particular, I'd like to thank Angela Sullivan, an ESL teacher at Enfield Primary School; Ben Smith, who in 1999 was a promotions officer for the South Australian Cricket Association; Graham Dodd, the enthusiastic coach of the Black Forest Primary School First XI, his son James ('Doddie'), who played in that team in 1999, and the other players who allowed me to watch their matches and ask them a lot of dumb questions. I'm particularly grateful to Bill 'Swampy' Marsh, who guided me through the final match, read the entire manuscript, made valuable suggestions and corrected many mistakes.

I read a lot of books as part of my research and lifted ideas here and there. Alan Border's *Beyond Ten Thousand: My Life Story* (Souvenir Press, 1994) was particularly inspiring. It was the young Alan who first played with green grapefruit from the backyard tree in lieu of proper cricket balls, and who crashed through the fibro roof of the family carport while fielding. The character of Clarrie 'Spinner' McGinty was inspired by Jack Iverson, the subject of Gideon Haigh's excellent biography *Mystery Spinner* (Text, 1999), but he is not intended to represent that extraordinary cricketer.

Finally, my thanks go to Kay Ronai and Helen Chamberlin, experts at both editing manuscripts and encouraging authors.

www.ruthstarke.itgo.com

Thomas C. Lothian Pty Ltd
132 Albert Road, South Melbourne, Victoria 3205

National Library of Australia
Cataloguing-in-publication data:

Starke, Ruth
NIPS XI.

ISBN 0 7344 0113 2.

I. Title.

A823.3

Illustrations by Gregory Rogers Studio
Cover design by Jo Waite
Book design by Paulene Meyer
Printed in Australia by Griffin Press

1

'Spring rolls and satays,' exclaimed Mr Drummond heartily. '*De*licious!'

Fried rice and noodles, thought Lan gloomily. *Bor*ing!

'Our International Food Day is always popular, of course,' Mr Drummond went on. 'But there's more to Multicultural Week than food. Here at North Illaba we have students from twenty-four different countries.'

The principal paused, as if anticipating a round of applause, or at least a surprised gasp or two. None came, so he plunged on. 'Some of you have been part of the school community for a number of years. Some of you are new arrivals. Multicultural Week is to let you all know just how special you are.'

He looked around the crowded classroom and smiled in an encouraging way. Most of the students smiled back politely, even those who understood very little of what he was saying. Lan, who understood every word, didn't smile. Was Multicultural Week supposed to make him feel special? It just made him feel different.

'During Multicultural Week we celebrate our *ethnic diversity*,' Mr Drummond said. He pronounced the last two words loudly and slowly. Lan waited for him to write them on the blackboard. He did, in large round letters which he underlined.

Behind him, Lan could hear Ms Trad translating for those whose grasp of English didn't yet extend to words like *ethnic diversity*.

'The celebrations are held in the last week of term, which may seem a long time away,' Mr Drummond continued. 'In the meantime, however, I'd like you to start thinking about how you can all contribute to making the week a success. Apart from your delicious national foods, that is.'

Last year Lan's mother had made 150 spring rolls and sold every one. Izram's mother had made *vadais*, little rissoles of lentils and peas, which had sold pretty well considering they were healthy. Hiroki's father had made sushi, which had hardly sold at all. Ethnic diversity was all very well, Lan concluded, but most people only wanted to eat what they were used to. Not him, of course. He put up his hand.

'Yes, Lan?'

'Will there be Australian food this time, sir?'

'Australian food?' Mr Drummond looked puzzled.

'Like pies and sausage rolls and lamingtons and stuff like that, sir?'

Mr Drummond gave a snort that made the vigorous grey hairs sprouting from his nostrils quiver. 'There wouldn't be much point, would there? You can get food like that every day of the week in the canteen.'

Well, *you* might be able to, Lan thought. His mother would as soon give him money to buy a meat pie for lunch as hand over $100 and tell him to blow it all on video games. He longed to hold a pie in his hand, like the skips did, and consume it in four huge bites without the meat and sauce dribbling down your chin.

'And then there's our Multicultural Concert,' the principal went on with renewed enthusiasm. 'Who took part last year?' A sprinkling of hands. 'Good! You know the kind of thing then.'

Lan did, and his heart sank. He'd have to wear an *ao dai* instead of his usual jeans and school jumper. He'd have to prance around on stage doing something traditionally Vietnamese. He was hopeless at it and he felt silly. There'd be Thai dancing and Cambodian singing. People would try to play 'Waltzing Matilda' on Chinese mouth organs and wave ribbons and do lion dances and sing Cambodian songs. All the usual stuff. The best thing in last year's concert was when the flames kept going out in the Indonesian Candle Dance, and Mrs Alfatih had dashed on stage waving a cigarette lighter and accidentally set fire to Aryo's hair.

He laughed aloud at the memory.

Mr Drummond's eyes swivelled towards him. 'Yes, Lan? You find the idea of a concert amusing?'

'No, sir. I mean, yes, sir.'

What was the right answer? Wasn't a concert meant to be amusing? And then, because the principal's eyebrows had snapped together in an ominous way, Lan said quickly, 'I just thought it would be good to do something different this year.'

Too late he remembered that the Multicultural Concert had been Mr Drummond's idea. Mr Drummond enjoyed popping into rehearsals and giving motivational pep talks to the performers. He especially enjoyed getting up on stage at the end of the concert and making his We Are One But We Are Many speech. No wonder Mr Drummond was looking at him like that.

'I'm always open to suggestions, Lan,' Mr Drummond said, looking anything but open. 'What did you have in mind?'

Lan had nothing in mind. But if he didn't come up with something, he'd find himself dancing on stage in an *ao dai* again. 'What I have in mind,' he said, trying to strike a mysterious note, 'is … um … well, it's a pretty big idea, sir. Something that would be fun and different, and it would be multicultural as well as Australian, but really cool, and the whole school could come. And parents.' Good one, Lan, he told himself. You haven't a clue what you're describing and now you've told the principal his multicultural concert sucks.

'It sounds *most* intriguing,' said Mr Drummond with a tight smile. 'Tell us more about it.'

Everyone in the classroom was looking at him now, even those who were still struggling with the concept of ethnic diversity.

'Er, I still have a few details to work out,' Lan said. He gave a few reassuring little nods as if tucked away inside his brain, lacking only a few finishing touches, was an almost completed blueprint for the greatest multicultural event the school had ever staged.

'Well, when you're a little more advanced in your planning, come and see me. I look forward to hearing all about your Big Idea.' He made the last two words sound as if they were written with capital letters. 'Thank you, Ms Trad.' With a regal wave of the hand, and a sharp look at Lan, the principal left the room.

'What was all that about?' Izram asked him, as they pushed their way out of the classroom.

Behind him, Ms Trad called his name and fluttered her hand at him, but the last thing Lan wanted was to get into a long discussion about Multicultural Week. Ignoring her, he headed out into the playground, Izram running to catch up.

'I didn't know you were so interested in celebrating Multicultural Week,' Izram panted, as they settled themselves on a corner of the oval. Lunchbreak was nearly over so there was little point in trying to join in any of the games. Not that Izram had any breath left. He fanned himself with the hat everybody was supposed to wear outside.

'I'm not. At least, not the way Drummo wants to celebrate it, with food days and a concert and all us ethnics in national costumes.'

'That's the way it's always celebrated. What else can we do?'

'All that SBS stuff,' Lan said. 'It's boring. Nobody even watches it on TV.'

Izram shrugged. 'Boring for us, maybe. We've done it all before. But some people have only just arrived in Australia. It makes them feel part of things, I guess.'

'It doesn't make me feel part of things. It makes me feel *a*-part. Separate. Like I'm not a real Australian. There's the *real* Aussies, the Anglos, the skips, and then there's us. We look different, we eat different, we speak different, we sing and dance different.'

'That's what we're supposed to be celebrating,' Izram pointed out. 'Our differences.'

'I don't want to celebrate difference,' Lan said stubbornly. He tugged savagely at a patch of clover. 'Every day of the year we know we're different. We can't get away from it. I'd rather celebrate sameness.'

Izram looked puzzled. 'How do you do that? What's it even mean?'

Lan wasn't sure how you'd celebrate it, but he

knew what he meant. 'Take a look around,' he said. 'What do you see?'

Izram, who had been sprawled on his stomach on the grass, propped himself up on one elbow, and looked. On the perimeters of the oval, the corrugated-iron roofs of the classrooms were shining in the heat, and he put up a hand to shield his eyes.

'Some guys kicking a ball. Some throwing a fris-bee. Girls walking around and talking. People sitting, hanging around. Loonies doing some crazy dance. A couple of teachers. Grass, sky, bike racks. I don't know, what am I supposed to be seeing?'

'Just that,' said Lan, triumphantly. 'Exactly what you said you saw. Get it?'

'No. Get what?'

'Listen, you didn't say the Cambodians are over there doing tai chi, and the Italians are kicking a soccer ball, and the Chinese are flying kites, did you?'

'Are they?' Izram, astonished, screwed up his eyes and peered into the distance.

'Course they're not, you geek. That's my point. Everyone's mixing in and doing the same sort of stuff. Look, Andy just kicked that soccer ball. Reckon they play soccer in Malaysia?'

'Dunno,' Izram said.

Lan didn't either. 'Well, Akka's there, too. I bet Arabs don't play soccer. They couldn't in those long robes they wear. They'd trip over, wouldn't they?'

'Or get bogged in the sand.'

'Right.'

The siren blasted for return to class.

'So what's your point?' Izram said. 'Okay, at school everyone mixes and does the same things, mostly. But it's different at home, isn't it? We have different customs, you just said so.'

'And that's why they'll never call us Australians. I'll always be a Nip. You'll always be a Paki. If we want them to see us as Aussies we've got to live like them and not be so different.'

They got to their feet as the soccer players came running past.

Andy Chen banged him on the back and laughed. 'Hey, it's the Multiculti Kid!'

Lan socked him on the upper arm. 'Cut it out.'

'No, listen, that was pretty cool, standing up to Drummo like that. It's about time we did something different. What's your Big Idea?'

'A celebration of sameness,' Izram said, before Lan could reply.

Andy nodded. 'Cool.' They walked together towards the classrooms. 'So what's that mean?'

'It means doing something that shows we're not different but the same.'

'That's not being *multi*cultural. That's being *mono*-cultural. We'd have to call it Monocultural Week,' Andy said. 'Drummo wouldn't go for that. Everyone wandering around being the same. It wouldn't be any different from every other week of the year, so how would anyone know we were even celebrating something?'

Lan kicked a stone and sent it scuttling across the bitumen. Andy had a point. Well, he could afford to be generous. 'Okay, the food can be multi, but there ought to be something mono. Something to show that we're Australian too.'

'Like what?' Izram asked.

'Something they do that we don't.'

'Um … something *they* do and we don't.' Andy squinted and looked skyward, as if seeking heavenly inspiration. 'Sheep shearing!' he suddenly exclaimed. He dug Izram in the ribs. 'Nobody in my family's ever sheared a sheep. How about yours, Iz?'

Izram shook his head. 'Not in Australia.' He thought some more. 'Probably not in Pakistan either.'

'We could truck 'em in from the country and fill the gym with bales of hay.'

'How about a corroboree?' Izram suggested. 'Maybe Drummo would let us light a fire on the oval.'

'Yeah! After we sheared the sheep we could cut 'em up and chuck the chops on a barbie. You can't get more Oz than that.'

'And throw boomerangs!'

The two of them cackled together.

Lan thumped both of them. 'Think you're pretty funny, don't you?' But he was grinning.

'Hey, don't listen to us,' Andy said, when he'd

calmed down. 'You're the one with the Big Idea for Multicultural Week. What is it?'

'I haven't got one,' Lan admitted.

'But you told Drummo —'

'Yeah.'

'Half the school's already talking about it,' Andy said. 'Everyone on the oval was talking about your Big Idea and trying to guess what it was.'

Lan knew that had to be a typical Andy exaggeration. Okay, so perhaps five people had happened to mention his Big Idea while they kicked a ball around. By going-home time, ten people might have heard. They'd talk about it on the school bus and by tomorrow morning maybe most of his class would have heard. By recess time it would have spread down the corridor and out to the playground. They'd finally hear about it in the staffroom — the teachers were always the last to hear about anything. Ms Trad would call him in and Mr Drummond would ...

He took a deep breath to calm himself. The world was full of Big Ideas. He'd come up with one.

'It'd better be good,' Andy said.

'I'll think of something,' Lan said.

But what?

2

The answer came to him on the side of a bus.

Lan had endured a tense couple of days evading the eager clutches of Ms Trad and going out of his way to avoid being seen by Mr Drummond. The latter had been especially hard on his nerves, not to mention his bladder.

The principal had a habit of standing at the window and gazing westwards at random moments throughout the day. The object of his gaze was generally thought to be a particularly fine row of flowering oleanders that bordered the toilet block. A group of concerned parents had wanted the poisonous trees cut down, but the possibility of dead pupils strewn across the bitumen had not been enough to persuade Mr Drummond to remove them. Nobody was quite sure whether he stood at the window admiring the blaze of pink and purple, checking for small bodies, or alert to possible raids by axe-wielding parents. Nevertheless, Lan had thought it wise to stay away from the toilet block as much as possible.

Coping with a full bladder while fending off questions and ignoring jokes had not been easy. Andy's label, The Multiculti Kid, had caught on and rumours swept the playground: Lan Nguyen was organising a camel race on the oval, or dragon-boat races at the Illaba public pool, or sumo wrestling in the school gym. Possibly all three.

They all missed the point, of course. But the thing that depressed Lan the most was that all their ideas were better than anything he'd been able to come up with. He was almost ready to accept defeat.

And then the answer trundled right past him at the bus stop.

When would you give up? And next to the question, the spiky blond hair, the clear green eyes, the wide grin, the smear of white zinc cream. *Just do it.* It was a terrific poster and the message struck him as powerfully as one of Warnie's leg-spinners.

Cricket. Shane Warne. The Waugh twins. The World Cup Winners. *Ozzie! Ozzie! Ozzie! Oy! Oy! Oy!*

Hadn't Melbourne given the champions a ticker-tape parade on their return home with the World Cup?

Hadn't 300,000 people lined the city streets to cheer them?

Hadn't the prime minister named Sir Donald Bradman as the Greatest Living Australian?

Wasn't Warnie about the biggest Oz sports hero in the whole world?

And wasn't cricket the greatest Anglo game of all?

Lan could feel a Big Idea forming in his brain. In fact, it was growing rapidly. He could feel it pushing against his forehead and trickling down his spine, eager to burst forth like one of those invasive creatures in *Alien*. If only Iz or Andy were standing with him at the No. 7 bus stop outside the Illaba Shopping Mall so he could tell them. If only he had a mobile so he could ring and tell them. If only he had a laptop so he could email Shane Warne.

Lan told himself to calm down. Before he proclaimed his Big Idea to the world, or at least to Mr Drummond, it needed a bit of fine-tuning. He needed to brainstorm. He needed to draw up a Working Plan. He needed more information. Where could he get it?

He looked around him. Not, he thought, in the Odd Spot Dry Cleaners or the Quicka Liqua shop or the Against the Grain bakery or any of the dozen other retail outlets in the mall. His eyes flicked over the two people waiting in the bus shelter with him: a girl with wild purple hair and an eyebrow ring who was wearing bike shorts and a leather jacket, and a woman with a heavy shopping bag who was wearing a harassed expression and smoking a cigarette. Neither looked as if they'd be much of an expert on cricket. Still, he could ask.

'Excuse me,' he said.

The girl ignored him. The woman turned her head.

'Do you know anything about cricket?' Lan said.

'Cricket?' She looked at him suspiciously. 'I barrack for the Crows.'

'That's football,' Lan said.

'Too right. Up the Crows.'

'What about cricket?'

'The Crows don't play cricket, love. You a little foreign student, are you?' She peered through her smoke at the logo on his school jumper and eyed the bag at his feet.

'No, I'm not,' Lan said. 'And I know the Crows don't play cricket.'

'Where are you from?' said the woman.

'Here. Illaba.'

'No, what country?'

'Australia,' Lan said.

'C'mon, with those eyes? You're not Australian. What country?'

'Listen,' Lan said, trying to stay cool. 'It's not important where I was born or where I came from. I'm here. This is my country. I live here. I'm Australian. Okay?'

The woman raised her eyebrows and shifted the shopping bag on her lap.

Lan looked away. He saw the bus coming. He stood up, partly to stand at the stop and partly to stop sharing the bench with the woman.

'I didn't think Nips played cricket,' the woman said, grinding out her cigarette butt.

The girl with purple hair suddenly came up beside him. 'You wanna know about cricket? Go over there, they'll tell you.' She pointed across the road.

The bus pulled to the kerb but not before Lan's gaze had taken in the sandstone buildings that faced the main street. The Illaba Council Chambers. The public library. And clearly visible at the end of the street that ran at right angles to them was the arched gate of the Illaba Memorial Oval.

Lan tried the council chambers first. There was nobody at the reception desk. He stood about for a while, wondering what to do. The silence and the red carpet and the walls covered with gilt-framed pictures of former lord mayors in red robes and gold chains were all a bit intimidating. There was a brochure rack near the entrance and he flicked through it. *Living With Arthritis. Living With A Disability. Coping with Blocked Drains. Disposing of Hazardous Wastes. Caring for Old Buildings. Caring for Old Relatives. Do You Have a Barking Dog? Why Are Adolescents Aggro? (Parent Easy Guide # 17)*. Nothing at all along the lines of *Do You Want to Play Cricket?*

'Cen I help yew, young man?'

Lan looked around. A woman in a red blazer with a gold logo on the breast pocket was addressing him from behind the reception desk. She wore pearl earrings and sounded just like the Queen when she made her Christmas speech. Lan wondered if she was the lady mayoress.

'Um ... I don't know,' he mumbled. He had a feeling he was in the wrong place.

'Rats, is it?'

'Sorry?'

'There's rawther a lot of them about rayt now. Are your parents rat payers?'

What was she talking about? What rats? Why would you pay rats? Or did she mean pay *for* rats? Lan felt himself getting angry again. Did she think Vietnamese people — *Nips* — ate rats? Lady mayoresses who spoke like the Queen ought to be better informed. He opened his mouth to tell her so.

'If they're rat payers, you see, there's no charge for the bait. It's all in there.' The woman nodded at the brochure Lan held in his hand. Lan, who hadn't realised he was holding anything, looked down at it. *Rodent Control: Advice for Ratepayers on Eliminating Rats and Mice.*

'Oh,' he said. 'Um, we haven't got rates. I mean rats. I was just looking for information —'

'Oh, a skewl project,' the woman said. 'In that case, you rally want the library, don't yew?'

Yes, Lan thought, he rally did.

Lan took a book from the pile in front of him. It was called *You Can Play Cricket!* He didn't recognise the name of the author — the blurb said he was 'an outstanding figure in the cricketing world' — but Lan liked that exclamation mark and the conviction of the title. In his mind he saw the Outstanding Figure striding through the book stacks, placing a firm hand on his shoulder and booming out ... how would he say it? '*You* can play cricket!' ... 'You *can* play cricket!' ... 'You can *play* cricket!' ... 'You can play *cricket*!' They all sounded good to Lan.

On the cover of the book was a photograph of two wildly excited young players, a wicket-keeper leaping in the air and a batter who had obviously just whacked the ball over the boundary, possibly over the grandstand roof. Both of them were Anglos. Lan flipped the pages. All the boys in the photographs batting, bowling and fielding were Anglos. The author's photograph inside the back cover showed him to be Anglo, too.

The bus-stop woman's voice echoed in his mind: *I didn't think Nips played cricket.* She had a point. He couldn't think of any who did either. He'd never heard of a Chinese or Japanese or Vietnamese cricket team. Where were the Filipino fast bowlers, the Cambodian medium pacers, the Thai spinners? That was the whole premise of his Big Idea, of course, but it was going to raise a few problems if there was a cricketing gene that only Anglos had.

Lan began to read the outstanding figure's introduction: *I first became interested in cricket at an early age when, like many boys, I received a cricket bat from*

*my parents as a birthday present. If they had given me
a football my life might have been totally different ...'*

And what if they'd presented you with a dictionary
and a pair of school shoes? That's what he'd been given
for his last birthday. His parents wanted him to speak
good English and look respectable. They would no
more have given him a cricket bat than a Tupac or
Public Enemy CD.

Dispirited, Lan continued reading. The library was
certainly stuffed with information about cricket. He'd
have to sit here until tomorrow midnight to get through
all the texts and tapes and videos. The library had
computers, too, some of them linked to the Internet.
There'd certainly be some good cricketing sites. Why
had he never come here before?

Actually, he had. He remembered now. During
Book Week last year his class had come to the library
to listen to some famous author who nobody but the
teacher had heard of. At the end of the session everybody had been given a borrower's card. His was still in
the side pocket of his school bag where it had remained
untouched ever since. So he wouldn't have to sit here
until tomorrow midnight, even supposing the library
would let him. He could borrow stuff and take it home.
Lan continued flipping through the titles: *Great
Australian Sports, Cricketers in the Making, How to
Play Cricket, My Life in Cricket, The Wit of Cricket* (a
skinny book and not likely to be useful; he put that one
aside). As he read and as the stack got lower, his spirits

began to rise. Perhaps it was nothing to do with race or genes, after all. Well, only indirectly.

It seemed to him that to be a good cricketer, to even understand the game let alone be good at it, you had to be born into a cricketing family. Your dad had to take you to matches from the time you were old enough to hold a bat. You had to play the game in the backyard with your brothers and cousins, or on the beach in summer. You had to start playing while you were still in short pants — Mark Taylor's dad had taught him to play using a cork cricket ball in the family garage — and your mum or dad had to drive you to matches on the weekend. The TV set had to be permanently tuned to cricket all summer and you had to sit around it with the family, drinking and arguing about l.b.w.s and no balls, and cheering for Warnie.

Heck, nobody was more Anglo than Warnie. That blond hair, the tan, the grin, the way he didn't give a stuff. In India, he ate cheese sandwiches and baked beans. At home, he ate hamburgers and meat pies. No use inviting Warnie to International Food Day, Lan thought.

Of course, it probably helped if you had a bit of natural ability. If someone stepped up to the nets who bowled like Warnie or batted like Bradman, the selectors probably wouldn't care how slanty his eyes were. They'd hardly say 'Go away, Nips can't play cricket,' would they?

On the other hand — there was always an other

hand, his father was fond of telling him — how did you get to bowl like Warnie or bat like Bradman if you were ethnically diverse? His own house didn't have a back-yard, and even if it did, when would his dad play with him? At night, after the shop finally closed around nine o'clock? Sunday was the only day his dad didn't work and that was devoted to family and visiting. As for playing in the garage, his mother worked in theirs.

Because he'd missed all that growing-up-with-cricket stuff, did that mean he couldn't play cricket?

He put aside the famous fast bowler's auto-biography and picked up the first book he'd looked at, the one with the exclamation mark. His eye slid down the page in front of him. *If you enjoy cricket or even if you have never played before ...* That was him. *You are never too old to learn ...*

Lan took the book to the front desk, along with an Ian Chappell coaching video and one on Don Bradman, and presented his card.

The librarian's name badge said 'Grace'. Noting his choice, she said brightly, 'Season's almost here, isn't it?'

'What season?'

Her eyebrows went up. 'Cricket season, of course.'

'Oh. Right.' How dumb must he look, not even knowing that? He felt his cheeks redden.

She slid a video into its plastic case. 'Do you play?'

'Sort of. Sometimes.' Although nobody else in the world would call it cricket. Any second now she'd say

'I didn't know Nips played cricket'. No, she probably wouldn't say 'Nips'.

'Are you a batsman or a bowler?'

Something else he didn't know. He wished she'd stop asking him trick questions.

'Not sure,' he mumbled. Now she'd know he was a fraud. How could any real cricketer not know? How red were his cheeks?

'I bet you're a good all-rounder.' She smiled and her voice was kind as well as cheerful. She returned his card, and handed him his book and videos. 'Going to try out for selection?' Lan looked blank. 'Look over there.' She indicated a big board at the entrance where community announcements were posted.

Lan located the notice from the Illaba Cricket Club next to one for Pensioners Bingo Night ('Bring a plate' — Why, he wondered; didn't they have enough?) and a lost dog description ('Answers to Mugger'). The club would be fielding two junior teams this season; training started on the first Tuesday of the month. Selection trials would be held at the oval this Saturday morning.

Lan slid his library card into his pocket and found the rat-control brochure. He took a pencil from the side pocket of his bag and wrote down the details on the back.

3

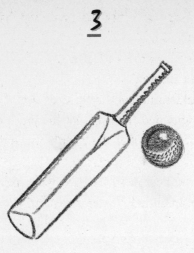

'Of course I know about cricket,' Izram said. 'I'm Pakistani.'

'I keep forgetting,' Lan said.

The two of them, as they often did after school, were sitting at a table in Izram's family's restaurant. From the kitchen wafted fragrant and spicy aromas of gently simmering curries. North Indian embroideries hung on the walls and brass trays gleamed. A painting of Mogul court ladies playing around a marble fountain hung on the wall. Mr Hussein, in the traditional *shalwar kameez* he always wore in the restaurant, was polishing glasses and cutlery. And to their right, so close you could lean out and trace them with your finger, the words on the front window in gold: *Bukhara — North Indian cuisine — Fully Licensed Restaurant and Takeaway.*

Izram laughed. Only someone like Lan could forget he was a Paki.

'What's funny?' Lan asked.

'Doesn't matter.'

'Are Pakistanis good at cricket then?'

Izram widened his eyes, let his jaw fall open, and pretended to fall off his chair with amazement.

'So they are?' Lan pressed.

'Only the best in the world. Well, second best this year,' Izram amended, remembering that painful World Cup loss.

'Why don't you play then?'

'I used to.'

'When?'

'When I was a little kid.'

'So why don't you play now?'

Izram shrugged. He didn't want to tell the reason, not even to Lan.

'But you'd play in this team, wouldn't you, Iz? We'd have to have some people who were good.'

'I didn't say I was *good*.'

'You said Pakis were good at cricket. I thought that meant all Pakis.'

'Listen, you dicko, if I said Aussies were good at swimming, that wouldn't mean everyone in the whole country —'

'Onion bhajis!' announced Mr Hussein, banging a plate down. He always gave them something good to eat. And he'd obviously overheard their conversation.

'*All* Pakistanis are good at cricket,' he said firmly. 'All of them. Even those who don't play. If they did play, they'd be good, like everyone else in the country.'

Lan wasn't going to argue, not when onion bhajis were on offer, but he was curious. 'Why?' he asked.

'Why are Pakistanis so good? Because we grow up with a bat and ball. We play cricket in the street from when we are tiny babies. Our arms and muscles grow strong and our eyes become sharp. So we make great warriors and brilliant cricketers. Hah!'

Mr Hussein clapped Lan on the back so heartily that a piece of onion bhaji flew out of his mouth and landed on the red tablecloth.

'But why do you play *cricket*?' Lan asked, wiping his mouth. He still hadn't got to the bottom of this mystery. 'Why not soccer or baseball?'

'They're not English games,' Mr Hussein said, as if that explained everything. He saw Lan's puzzled expression. 'You've heard of the British Raj, yes? For two hundred years the British ruled India. They came here, too, to Australia and New Zealand, and to the West Indies, Sri Lanka and South Africa. Everywhere they went they took their language and their law and their afternoon tea and their boiled mutton and puddings. And their cricket!'

Lan moved sideways to dodge the thump. If the British had colonised Vietnam instead of the French, his dad would have learnt the game. His dad would have taken him to matches and bought him a cricket bat for his birthday. There might now be a Vietnamese team playing Test cricket. How funny.

'So are you boys going to play this summer? Try for the school First XI, hey?'

'Our school doesn't play cricket,' Izram reminded him.

'I forgot. What stupidity!' Mr Hussein shook his head sadly at the folly of so-called educators.

'I'm putting a team together,' Lan said.

'Splendid!' cried Mr Hussein. 'Izzie will be your opening batsman. Who else is on the team?'

'I don't know yet,' Lan admitted. 'I only got the idea just now.'

'It's Lan's Big Idea for Multicultural Week,' Izram put in.

'A cricket match?'

The boys nodded.

'Against whom?' Mr Hussein asked.

Lan's face fell. It was a good question. Why hadn't he thought of it? As Iz had reminded his father, North Illaba wasn't a cricketing school. There was football and netball and that was it. There was no North Illaba First XI to play against. If he took his Big Idea to the principal, Mr Drummond would point this out to him. He'd go away feeling like an idiot. And they'd be back to Vietnamese dancing.

'What's the nearest school to us?' he asked. 'A school that plays cricket?'

'King's,' Izram replied.

Lan nodded.

King's College was less than five kilometres from North Illaba and shared the same bus route. But that was the only common meeting ground. King's students wore smart navy blazers and striped ties. They carried personal laptops and mobile phones. They swam in their indoor swimming pool and competed in the Head of the River. Of course they played cricket. Lan had seen them on the bus in their glamorous white sweaters, tall confident boys with loud voices and light-coloured eyes that looked straight through you. They spread themselves possessively over the rear seats and cluttered the aisle with their large sports bags.

'King's First XI won the Intercollegiate Cup last year,' Izram said. 'And the year before. Two of the play-ers in the state team come from King's.'

Mr Hussein looked doubtful. 'Perhaps you are aiming a bit high,' he said.

'I want to aim high,' Lan said.

'Well, you must go down to the Illaba Cricket Club,' Mr Hussein said. 'The season will be starting soon. Register your team and the club will include you in the schedule of matches. Then all you do is play hard and work yourself up the ladder until you are cham-pions. That is how it works in Lahore.' He took the empty plate and went off to the kitchen.

Lan remembered the information he had scribbled on the back of the rat brochure. He got it out of his pocket.

'Your dad's right, Iz. Look, I wrote it down. We ought to go to these training sessions and coaching thingos, whatever they call them.'

'Clinics.'

'And we should register our team and start playing.'

'What team? We don't have a team.'

Lan took out his pencil. 'Let's get things in the right order.' He wrote: *1. Pick a team*.

'Select,' said Izram.

'What?'

'You don't pick a team you *select* a team.'

Lan made the correction. Best to do things right from the very start. It was a good thing Iz knew what was what. Imagine if he'd told the boss of the Illaba Cricket Club, or even Mr Drummond for that matter, that he'd *picked* his team.

Then he wrote: *2. Go to session at cricket club Saturday*.

'Maybe we should do that the other way round,' Izram said.

'Why?'

'Well, how can we select a team if we don't see them in action first?'

Lan considered. If he'd thought about it at all, he'd imagined that once the news got out that he was forming a cricket team, ten players would just present themselves. He'd be the eleventh, of course.

He told Izram this but Iz, who had watched a lot

of cricket, said it didn't work like that. You didn't take just anyone. A team had to have a couple of good opening batsmen, three stroke players, at least one all-rounder, a good wicket-keeper, and a variety of bowlers: fast, medium and spin.

Lan frowned. 'But what do we do if six spin bowlers want to join the team?'

From behind the bar they heard Mr Hussein laughing at something.

Izram said, 'Let's just see who wants to play.'

4

How did word about his Big Idea get about? Lan didn't know. He had only told Izzie and Izzie's dad and Andy Chen, who happened to sit next to him on the bus to school the next morning.

Andy had said straight away that it was a great idea — 'better than sheep shearing, ha ha!' — and he'd be in the team. In Kuala Lumpur he'd gone to a British school but had never been selected for any of its cricket teams, not even the very bottom one.

'Why not?' Lan had asked.

Andy had shrugged. 'Chinese can't play cricket, I guess.'

Lan was reminded again of the bus-stop lady's comment. 'I don't think that's true. Anyway, we'll prove it's not true.' He lowered his voice, even though

Andy was sitting right next to him. 'Listen ... have you ever been called a Nip?'

'Yeah, lots of times. Haven't you?'

'Yeah. But I'm Vietnamese.'

'Anyone with slanty eyes is a Nip.'

'Oh,' Lan said. Then: 'Do you mind being called a Nip?'

Andy shrugged again. 'I don't care. It's better not to care. If you show you care, they've got you, haven't they?'

Lan thought about it. 'We could call our team that,' he said eventually.

'What?'

'The Nips.'

Andy laughed.

He hadn't had time to tell anyone else, but by morning recess the news had spread. Lan Nguyen was looking for ethnics who wanted to play cricket. Who would they play against? Nobody knew.

By lunchtime people were better informed. There would be an all-day cricket match and carnival on the school oval. The opposition would be the district champions, the undefeated King's College Junior XI. The town band would play. Shane Warne would present the winner's trophy. Mark Taylor and Steve Waugh would commentate for ABC radio. The match would be televised by Channel 9. There would be a special press box.

'Wow!' said Izram excitedly. 'Your idea is getting bigger and bigger!'

Others were more scornful.

'You are such a liar!' sneered Adam Morris. 'Radio and TV. As if!'

'You've never even met Shane Warne,' jeered Ryan West.

Lan didn't know whether to worry or feel pleased. It was good that his Big Idea was generating so much interest and excitement, but it was getting a bit out of hand. Very soon now Mr Drummond would hear about it and want to know all the details. That was the worry. Lan didn't have any details.

He did, however, have some names.

Akram Rajavi passed him a note in the middle of Geography which said 'Can I be in your criket team?'

Lan's first thought was to exclude anybody who couldn't even spell the name of the game. His second thought was that whatever Akka was, and Lan wasn't entirely sure, his eyes didn't slant so he probably wasn't a Nip. But he was certainly ethnically diverse.

He looked across the room at Akka's eager face and reminded himself that good spelling and the shape of your eyes had nothing to do with playing cricket. He nodded.

Akram beamed and gave him a thumbs up.

At least half a dozen people told him they'd like to be on the team. One was Hiroki, the only student in the school to have a laptop and a mobile. Lan thought that both would be very useful even if Hiroki proved to be hopeless at cricket. Another, Tomas, had been a surprise. Lan didn't think he could even speak English. He'd only been at North Illaba a couple of weeks and Lan couldn't remember ever talking to him. But he'd written his name on a piece of paper — Tomas Nunez — and shyly handed it to Lan.

'Cricket,' he said.

'Have you ever played the game?'

'Yes, please. Cricket.'

Had he understood? What did it matter?

Lan nodded and put the scrap of paper in his pocket. Tomas looked satisfied.

Not everybody's reaction was positive. Lan was standing by his locker, talking to Hiroki, when Adam, Ryan and others in the lunchtime ball-kickers squad came streaming in from the oval.

'Hey, if it isn't the Multiculti Kid!'

'Nah, it's Steve Waugh! See the baggy green?'

'Don't think much of your Big Idea, but.'

'You gunna play cricket too, Hiroki?'

'Thought Nips couldn't play cricket?'

'They can't. That's why they have to form their own team. Nobody else'll have 'em!'

They hooted with laughter.

'Any of you can be in the team,' Lan said. 'If you're a good enough cricketer, that is.'

'Bad enough, you mean,' jeered Adam.

'We're Australians,' Ryan said. 'We wouldn't want to be in a loser team of Nips.'

They sauntered off down the corridor.

By the end of the day it seemed every kid in the school had heard of the Big Idea. As Lan had feared, it then reached the ear of Mr Drummond.

'The principal would like to see you before you go home today, Lan.' His class teacher looked up from the note that had just been handed to her at the door.

'Ooooohhh!' A mass murmur of mock apprehension ran around the room.

'Howzat!' called someone from the back, and people giggled. Probably Ryan, Lan thought. He was getting a bit fed up with Ryan West.

Izram kicked the back of his chair. 'Want me to come with you?'

'Would you?'

'Sure.'

How many kids in the school would go and see Drummo when they didn't have to? Izzie was a real mate, Lan thought gratefully. And it would look better if there were two of them. More ... what was the word? He couldn't think of the word. The one that meant they'd look like they knew what they were doing.

At least he could go to the toilet now.

'What'll you tell him?' Izram asked when they found themselves outside Mr Drummond's door.

Lan noted the use of the singular pronoun. 'You' not 'we': obviously Izram expected him to do all the talking. He tried to look confident and unconcerned. 'Depends on what he asks me, doesn't it?'

'He'll ask you about your Big Idea.'

'I know.'

'He'll ask you who's on the team.'

'I know.'

'He'll ask you what we're going to play with. And who we're going to play against. He'll ask you —'

'Jeez, Iz, stop telling me what he'll ask, okay?' Lan hissed. 'You're making me nervous.'

The door opened. It was Mr Drummond. 'What's going on out here? Oh, it's you, Lan. And ... Izram, isn't it? Right, well you can wait outside while this young man and I have a little chat.'

'Please sir, if it's about my multicultural idea then Iz is sort of in it too, sir.'

Mr Drummond looked from one to the other.

'Iz is helping me organise things, sir,' Lan said, pleased with the word *organise*, which had suddenly popped into his head. It certainly made him sound as if he knew what he was doing.

It seemed to convince Mr Drummond. 'All right. Come in. Shut the door.'

He sat down behind his desk. 'Pull up a chair,' he invited.

Lan and Izram looked at each other. Neither of them had ever been invited to sit down before.

'So,' Mr Drummond said when they were seated, 'what's this I hear about a cricket match?'

Lan took a deep breath. 'Well, this is my idea.'

When he'd finished, Mr Drummond sat clicking the top of his ballpoint in and out without saying anything. Then he got up and went to the window and gazed out at the boy's toilet block. Or possibly the oleander bushes.

'You don't yet have a team,' he said, without turning his head.

'But I've got heaps of names,' Lan said. 'We will have a team.'

'Some of whom have never played cricket before, correct?'

Lan admitted this was probably true.

'And you have no pitch on which to play?'

'We will have when we register our team with the Illaba Cricket Club,' Izram put in.

'This team you don't yet have?'

Why did he keep on about that, Lan thought crossly. If he'd given him a couple of extra days, if he hadn't been so quick to haul him in for a little chat, he'd have had a team. Here's our opening batsmen, he could have said. Here's our wicket-keeper, our bowlers ...

'What about equipment? Bats, balls, gloves, those helmet things. Can't expect the school to pay for all that, you know.'

Mr Drummond was good at thinking of things

they hadn't thought about, Lan admitted. 'And a coach?' Mr Drummond turned around. 'Who's going to coach this team you don't yet have?'

The boys exchanged glances. 'The club has coaching clinics every week,' Izram said.

'You don't think you might need more than that?'

They didn't answer.

'Who will you play against?'

'We thought King's,' Lan said.

'King's?' Mr Drummond said incredulously.

'They've got a good team,' Izram said.

'They've never been beaten,' Lan added.

'And naturally you thought this would be the ideal team for you to play against,' Mr Drummond said.

'We thought we'd have a go,' Lan said.

'We'll work up to them,' said Izram. 'We wouldn't play them straight off.'

The principal had a big planning calendar on his wall. He walked across to it and beckoned. 'Come here.' He pointed. 'Here we are today. And here ...' his pen tracked across and down 'is the start of Multi-cultural Week.'

The two dates weren't far apart at all. Less than ten centimetres, Lan calculated.

'That should give us plenty of time,' he said.

Mr Drummond's eyebrows came together like two caterpillars as he tried to decide whether Lan was being cheeky or not. No, he wasn't. The boy was just stupid. Did he really imagine he could put a cricket team together in the time available, let alone one which could hold its own against the King's First XI?

'Multicultural Week is an important tradition at North Illaba and I'm afraid I can't commit the school to pie in the sky,' he said.

What was Drummo on about now, Lan wondered. Neither he nor Iz had even mentioned pies. There ought to be pies, of course. Australians all ate pies when they went to watch sport. 'In the sky' must refer to eating them in the grandstands. Mr Drummond didn't seem to like that idea.

Lan suddenly remembered how cross the principal had been that day he'd asked if there'd be meat pies at International Food Day. He seemed to have a thing about pies. Okay, no pies.

'The food would be international, of course,' he said reassuringly.

'Ah!' said Mr Drummond. He looked thoughtful. 'Yes, I see what you're getting at. All on the same day, eh?' The boys could have their little game of cricket on the oval — who'd be interested, apart from their parents? — but with some international food stands, perhaps a spot of ethnic music and dancing during the lunchbreak ... Yes, it might work.

He strode back to his desk and picked up his desk diary. 'I'll probably live to regret this but I'm prepared to give you two weeks. If you've got your team and everything organised by then, I'll agree. Fair enough?'

'Thanks, Mr Drummond!' Lan and Izram grinned at each other. They made for the door and freedom.

'I want names! I want hard facts!' the principal called after them. 'I want to know who and what and when and where, understand? Down to the last detail!'

'Yes, Mr Drummond.'

Out in the corridor they gave each other a high five.

Easy-peasy!

5

Izram was probably right, Lan thought. Better not to select the team until after Saturday's training session. In the meantime, it wouldn't hurt to make sure everybody was playing by the same rules. Their experience varied widely. And their knowledge.

This soon became evident at the meeting Lan called to announce the successful outcome of his Big Idea. It was held the day after the meeting with Mr Drummond. About twenty-five attended, including a few girls.

'Sorry,' Lan said. 'Cricket's a man's game.'

'Then how come the Australian women's cricket team is the world champion?' demanded Lisa Huynh.

'Because they play *separately*,' Izram retorted. 'Go and form your own team.'

Grumbling, they departed.

They got rid of Ms Trad just as rapidly.

'There may be some language difficulties, Lan. I should stay and translate.'

'We'll be okay, Ms Trad. We're only talking cricket, not rocket science.'

Now he thought he might have been a little too optimistic. For some of those present, one subject seemed as mysterious as the other.

'There's a lot of things I don't understand about cricket,' said Hiroki. 'How do they score? What's a wrong-un? What are they looking for when they get down on their knees and stare at the pitch?'

'Why do they rub the ball, you know, down there? It looks rude.'

'For good luck.'

'It's to make the ball swing,' corrected Izram. 'If one side of the ball is smooth and shiny and the other side is rough and dull, the ball swings when you throw it.'

'But it's such a slow game! One side mostly sits in the stands waiting and the other side stands around on the oval for hours doing nothing.'

'They're not doing nothing, they're fielding. Anyway, that's only in Test cricket,' said Izram. 'One-day cricket is a much faster game.'

'Faster? Yeah, like a horse and cart is faster than walking.'

'Sometimes they play for days and still nobody wins,' someone said.

'Yeah, why are the scores so hard to understand? It's never simple like soccer. If the score is Bologna 3, Juventus 1, you know straight away who won.'

That was Sal Catano. Lan wondered why he had come to the meeting. Italians played soccer, didn't they? He'd never heard of an Italian cricketer.

'Why do they yell "Howzat!" and throw their arms in the air and jump up and down?' asked Jemal. 'Is it like a war cry?'

'Where's the silly point?'

'Wherever you're standing, dumbo!'

Lan rapped on a desk. 'Izzie knows all about cricket. Iz, explain the rules to everyone.'

'I don't think I know all the rules,' said Izram, looking worried.

'Not all the rules, you geek. Just *the* rules. And be quick. We haven't got all day.'

Everyone looked at him expectantly.

Izram cleared his throat. 'Well, there are two sides, eleven in each. The captains toss and one team goes out in the field and the other goes in. That's an innings, okay? Each player in the side that's in goes out to bat, and the bowler tries to get him out and when he's out he comes in, and the next player goes in until he's out. Then when they're all out, that's the end of that innings. The side that's been out in the field comes in, and the other team goes out and tries to get out the ones coming in. That's the next innings. Sometimes there are still players in and not out. Then when both sides have been in and out, including the not outs, that's the end of the game. The team with the most runs wins.'

There was silence.

'Anyone got a question?' asked Lan.

They looked dazed, as if there were so many questions running around inside their minds it was impossible to narrow it down to just one.

Finally, Akram spoke. 'This may sound dumb, but when they go in, where *is* in? I don't get it.'

'Look, we've all got some homework to do,' said Lan. His head was spinning, too. Trust Izram to confuse everyone. 'You can't expect to learn everything about the game in five minutes. Check out the Illaba Library. It's got heaps of books and videos and there's a lady there called Grace who knows heaps about cricket.'

'There's some cool sites on the Net, too,' added Izram.

Hiroki raised his hand. 'How are you going to pick the team?'

'Iz will help me *select* the team,' said Lan. 'That's why everyone who wants to play has to come to the Illaba Cricket Club on Saturday morning. We only want serious players. Players who will come to training and coaching and practice. It'll take a lot of hard work.'

'It'll be tough,' warned Izram. 'Really, *really* tough. You'll be pounding up and down the oval at dawn. You'll be catching and throwing and running and jumping. You'll be batting and bowling till your arms fall off. You'll be sweating blood!'

Several people looked alarmed. Lan felt a little alarmed himself. If Izram scared them all off they wouldn't have a team.

'On the other hand,' he said quickly, 'if you play cricket you won't have to be in the Multicultural Concert. And you know what those rehearsals were like last year.'

They did. Suddenly sweating blood didn't seem so bad.

'That went okay,' said Izram when the meeting was over. He ran an eye down the list. 'I reckon we've got at least twenty names.'

'They won't all stick it,' said Lan. 'You wait; some of them won't even show up on Saturday.'

It occurred to him that unless he did some persuasive talking at home he might be one of them. In his family, Saturday was just another working day and cricket was a game that foreigners played.

Lan's mother had escaped from Vietnam with her younger sister and brother. With about fifty other people, they had sailed in a small boat to Indonesia. It had taken seven days to get there and there was little food or water. They had spent over a year in a refugee camp, where she had met Lan's father. Then they had all come to Australia.

Lan had first heard the story when he was about six. 'Why did you leave Vietnam?' he had asked.

'Because of the war and the Communists, because people were being shot in the streets,' his mother had said.

He didn't know what Communists were but it sounded exciting. Nobody ever got shot in Dunrobin Street.

'We would hide under the tables when the shooting started. Sometimes it would go on for two or three hours.'

His face had lit up. At six, hiding under the table was still one of his favourite games.

'It wasn't fun, believe me,' his mother said.

It seemed like pretty good fun to Lan. 'Did you and Grandma have guns?'

'Guns! Of course not. We were very scared. When the shooting stopped we would come out of hiding and find blood and bodies lying in front of the house.'

It sounded thrilling. The only thing he had ever found dead in Dunrobin Street was a cat. And before he'd had a good look, Mr Lee from across the road had scraped it up with a shovel.

'Why did Grandma Mai stay behind in Vietnam?' he'd asked.

'She thought that if we all left together and got caught, there would be no family to help us. So we went first, and she stayed.'

Lan was sad then, because she had died before she

could be reunited with her children in Australia. So he had never met his grandmother. Her photo was kept in the family shrine in a corner of the living room. They put flowers in front of it and burnt incense. On special days they put a bowl of rice soup and fruit there, to honour her memory.

Family was more important than anything else. Much more important than playing games. He'd known that since he was six years old.

6

'Will you explain to Dad about Saturday morning? That I have to go to cricket training?'

'Why is this so important to you?' his mother asked.

'Because I'm the organiser. I told you. We have to select the team.'

'Yes, I understand. But why cricket? It's a foreign game.'

Lan dropped his school bag on the floor of the garage. Here we go again, he thought. His mother was so predictable. 'It's not foreign here, Ma. Here it's an Australian game. Australian cricketers are the World Cup champions.'

'So you think you might be a world champion, too?' His mother guided a white shirt sleeve through the sewing machine.

50

'Well, not right away,' Lan conceded modestly. But in two or three years, who knew?

'Nobody in our family ever played cricket,' his mother said.

'No? I thought you told me Grandma Mai was leg-spinner for the Saigon First XI.'

'Don't be smart.'

'Well, that's such a dumb reason not to.'

His mother looked up and saw his face. 'It's not just the game. What about family duties after school and on weekend? What about your brother and sister? What about helping your father in the shop?'

'I'll look after them. I'll take them with me. I'll still help Dad.'

'How? When? At half-time? In between hitting goals?'

Lan sighed. A Vietnamese family was going to be a handicap. He bet Shane Warne hadn't had to lug little brothers and sisters along to cricket practice. He bet Shane Warne's mum had never asked him how many goals he'd hit. Mrs Warne would have been in the laundry washing his white shirts, not sewing them in the garage.

His mother dropped the shirt on top of the pile in the cardboard box near her feet. 'Ooof! That's enough.' She rubbed her eyes. 'I must get dinner.'

'So will you talk to Dad? Explain about this Saturday and everything?'

She stood up and stretched. 'Oh, my back!' Then

she made for the kitchen, through the side door of the garage.

Lan picked up his school bag and trailed after her. In the living room off the kitchen, the twins were bouncing on the sofa, while *Bananas in Pyjamas* rolled across the TV screen.

'Well, will you?' he repeated.

Linh gave her brother a shove and he rolled off the sofa. Tien looked surprised, then let out a roar.

'Explain? Explain what? That you want to play games, not study and help family? I don't think I can explain that very well. I think you have to explain that to your father.'

Lan thought it might be easier to explain the laws of motion to the twins.

By eight o'clock the twins were in bed and Lan was doing his homework. He always finished this long before dinner. Tonight, however, he'd decided it would be a good move if he was at the kitchen table, studying, when his father came home.

His mother was in the living room, watching TV. Even though her English was poor, Mrs Nguyen found many of the shows entertaining. She liked the life-style programmes best, especially the home-decorating ones that showed you how to erect a veranda in six minutes or how to transform your kitchen cupboards with chicken wire and silver paint. She always watched the cooking shows. At the moment, a fat lady was generously spreading jam and cream over three layers of chocolate sponge.

It made Lan feel hungry. He left the table to get himself a snack. When he came back, another fat lady was covering a joint of roast beef with bacon slices.

'I don't know why you watch,' he said. 'You never cook anything they show you.'

'I don't like foreign food,' his mother said.

In all the years he'd been friends with Izram, his parents had never eaten at the Bukhara. 'Why should we go there,' his mother had said, 'when there is good food at home?'

Lan munched his bread and decided he'd done enough study. He pushed his text books aside and reached for *You Can Play Cricket!* Already, he had read it from cover to cover. But there was so much to learn. He opened it at random and began reading about the forward defensive shot instead, *the basic shot on which all forward strokes in cricket are based* ...

He imagined himself playing cricket for Australia, striding proudly off the field having completed a superb innings, batting gloves in his hand. The crowd were rising to their feet and he was waving his bat in acknowledgement of the thunderous applause. Small boys reached out to touch him as he strode through the players' gate and TV crews from around the world clamoured for an interview. Tomorrow he would be headline news: "Nguyen saves Australia: 350 not out!"

He was just trying to work out why he was striding off the field if he was not out when he heard the old Datsun coming down Dunrobin Street. He waited until he heard the clunk as the muffler hit the drainage hump at the start of the driveway, then closed the book and slipped it back into the middle of the pile.

Lan's father owned a small mixed grocery near the central market. It was unusual for him to be home much before eight, and some nights it was much later. He looked tired when he came in the door, but he nodded with approval when he saw Lan.

'That's the thing! If you want to get a good job you have to study. Look at your mother and me. We do not have good jobs. We have some education but no qualifications. We work hard so that you have a better life.' Lan had heard the argument many times, but this was not a good time to hear it again. He jumped up and said, 'Would you like a cup of tea, Dad?'

'I would, yes. Thank you.' His father sat down at the table.

Lan switched on the kettle and rinsed the tea pot. How was he going to tell him about playing cricket? He would have to do it gently.

His father looked at the pile of textbooks. He picked up *Australian Society* and flicked through it.

Lan recognised a good opening when he saw it. 'That's all about our government and history and the way we live and the games we play and stuff like that,' he said.

His father grunted.

'Sport is so important in Australia, Dad, there's a whole chapter about it. Isn't that interesting?'

His mother called from the living room: 'He wants to play cricket! On Saturday.'

So much for the gentle approach, Lan thought.

'What's this?'

Uh-oh! His father had found the cricket book.

'Here's a nice cup of tea, Dad.'

'What is all this about playing cricket? Tell me.'

Lan did. His father listened and sipped his tea. Lan put special emphasis on how Mr Drummond had given him the *entire* responsibility for organising the team.

'Playing cricket will not make you a person of good money with a good job,' his father said when he had finished.

'I'll still study,' Lan said. 'It's got nothing to do with my school work. Anyway, Shane Warne's a millionaire.'

'Shane Warne not Vietnamese.'

No argument there, Lan thought. 'So?'

'Vietnamese not have time to play cricket. Vietnamese work six days a week, from sunrise to sunset. Very little time free, very little energy.'

'But children have to play! Don't tell me children in Vietnam don't have time to play.'

'Of course they play. But they play simple games, like I did when I was a boy. They kick a can, they skip rope, they play marbles with stones.'

Whoopee, thought Lan. He was glad his parents had made their escape. 'But Linh and Tien watch *Sesame Street* and Wiggles videos,' he said. When they go to school they'll want to play netball and football and cricket, too, I bet. We live in Australia, Dad, not Vietnam.'

'How much will it cost?' his mother asked.

This was something Lan hadn't considered. 'I don't know. Not much. Why should it cost anything?'

'Playing sport always costs money,' his mother said. 'For a start, what will you play with?'

'The cricket club will have bats and pads and stuff.'

His father considered, his fingers making a drumming sound on the books. 'All right, you want to play sport. I agree. Physical education also important. I send you to tai chi lessons. How about that?'

Lan sighed. How to get his point across? 'Dad, that's a Nip sport.'

'Don't say that word!' his mother said sharply.

'Let ignorant foreigners say it if they must, but not you, please,' his father said.

'You two always call Australians foreigners but they're not,' Lan cried. 'We are. We're the foreigners! Ma won't cook the food on TV because she says it's foreign, but it's just normal English-type food. In this country Vietnamese and Indian and Chinese food is foreign food and tai chi is a foreign sport. All I want to do is to stop being a foreigner for a while and play an

Australian sport like cricket. And it's not fair if you won't let me!'

Lan stopped. He had gone too far. In some things he was Vietnamese, and Vietnamese children did not raise their voice or talk back to their elders. Now his father would say it was clear he was far too Australian already, and send him off to bed and that would be that.

There was silence. His father and mother looked at each other. His mother raised an eyebrow in that special way she had and his father gave a little shrug. They didn't say anything but they seemed to be communicating.

Then his father said quietly, 'Very well, if you want it so much. But school work must come first, then helping in family. Is this agreed?'

'Agreed,' Lan said, surprised and elated. Wow! He felt like leaping in the air and yelling, like Warnie did when he took a wicket.

'Now can I have dinner, please?' his father asked. 'Foreign food or Australian food, I'm too hungry to care.'

Lan grinned and scooped up the books from the kitchen table.

'And this one,' his father said, handing it to him.

'Thanks, Dad.'

Lan put it on top of the pile: *You Can Play Cricket!*

7

So many fathers. It was the first thing Lan noticed when he and Izram arrived at the Illaba Oval a little before ten. Cars lined the nearby streets, and boys and fathers milled around the entrance to the clubroom or sat on the lower steps of the grandstand. Several of the boys had brought their own cricket gear. Many appeared to know each other. None of them were Asian.

Then Andy and Akram and some of the others from school arrived. None of them were accompanied by fathers. Some, like Lan's, had to work on Saturday mornings. Akram hadn't even asked his father. 'He thinks cricket's feeble. He'd call me a mad Arab and tell me to mow the lawn instead.'

More arrived by the time the clubrooms opened and then some men in club blazers had appeared with bags of equipment. 'We'd like everyone to register first,' one of them called out. 'Line up, please!'

They formed a queue in front of a table where a man sat recording names. His face was round and red and he had a high shiny forehead and thinning sand-coloured hair. His brows and lashes were so fair they were almost invisible. He wore a badge which said 'Len Burridge, Club Secretary'.

'We're a team,' Lan said when it was his turn. 'There's about ten of us here so far but more might turn up.'

'We do the team selections, son,' the man said. 'That's what this is all about.'

'I know,' Lan said. 'But we're already in a team. We're just not sure who does what yet.'

'We'll let you know who does what after we see you do your stuff this morning.'

'Cool,' Lan said. 'Me and Iz were hoping you'd help us with that.'

Mr Burridge squinted at him in a puzzled sort of way. He pushed a list across the table. 'Write your details down here and take the number next to your name.'

'All of us?'

'Everyone who wants to try out.'

Lan wrote his name and age, his address and tele-phone number. Then he gave the list to Izram, who passed it on to Andy and then the others all wrote down their names: Hiroki, Akram, Jemal, Phon, Satria ... Lan was pleased so many had turned up.

Mr Burridge looked at them in some surprise. 'Where're you all from?'

Not again, thought Lan. *I didn't know Nips played cricket.* 'From round here,' he said, and took the bib with his number on it.

He and the others went out onto the oval. Lan made a quick count. About forty. All Anglos, he pointed out to Izram.

'There's one who's not. *And* he's got a cricket bag.' Izram gestured towards a tall boy in grey Adidas track pants and a white T-shirt who was standing a little apart from the group. Lan thought he might be Chinese.

A man who said he was the chairman of selectors of the Illaba Cricket Club welcomed them. He said how gratified he was to see so many boys interested in playing club cricket for Illaba, which had a proud and glorious history. The selectors were always on the look-out for new talent, and this morning they hoped to find it. Perhaps the next Shane Warne or Steve Waugh was standing right in front of him now.

Lan nudged Izram. 'That's us.'

The chairman introduced the men with the clip-boards, the ones who'd be looking for the new talent. 'Play hard this morning, but enjoy yourself, too,' the chairman said.

Then the coach took over. He had a loud bossy voice and a freckled, peeling nose. He wore a whistle on a ribbon around his neck, and he fiddled with it as he bounced lightly up and down on the balls of his feet. He began by telling them what they were going to do this morning. Suddenly he stopped. 'You two boys chatting over there,' he said, frowning. 'I've got one Golden Rule: when I talk you don't. You pay attention and shut up.'

Lan shifted his position to see who he was ticking off. One was Tomas. He didn't know the other boy.

The boy's face reddened. 'We are. I was just telling him —'

'Didn't you hear what I just said?' the coach interrupted. 'I don't care what you were talking about. No talking when I talk, that's the rule.'

'I was telling Tomas what you said,' the boy said. 'He doesn't speak English too good. If I don't tell him he won't understand what's going on.'

The coach looked taken aback. He glanced across at the chairman who gave a slight shrug. The coach said, 'Er, right then. Let's do a warm-up.'

They did star jumps and leg stretches and arm circles. After only ten minutes Lan was so warmed up he had to take off his jumper. Izram, just as sweaty and red in the face, kept his tracksuit top on.

Then they ran around the oval and did a lot of throwing and catching. Or throwing and dropping, as it more often was. They bowled at stumps and then put on gloves and took it in turns to crouch down behind the wicket and take imaginary stumpings.

'Keep your eye on the ball!' the coach yelled.

'I would but it zooms past my head before I see it,' Hiroki muttered to Lan. 'Don't make me wicket-keeper, will you?'

Izram, on the other hand, found he had a talent for it. He liked the way the ball came into the gloves with a sweet soft thud, and he liked the fact that it came there with a minimum of effort on his part. Running around the oval had nearly killed him.

Lan was eager to try bowling. In his mind was a vision of the great bowlers he had seen on the Ian Chappell coaching video. The fast ones did a long run up before letting the ball fly. When it was his turn he took the ball and trudged off towards the horizon.

The coach called him back. 'You're not runnin' a marathon,' he barked. 'Start where you can at least see the wicket.'

There had been giggles from some of those watching. Lan went red with embarrassment. With little idea of what he was doing, he started off on the wrong foot, his run-up was full of stammers and stutters, and he released the ball too late. It dribbled away, nowhere near the wicket.

The next bowler, a tall boy with fair hair and a gold chain round his neck, had given him a superior look, and from a smooth running stride had sent down a top spinner that rattled the stumps.

'Nice one, Macca!' His two friends, both of whom had blond hair, applauded vigorously. One said loudly, 'Some real losers here today.'

'Can't catch, can't bowl,' said the second blond.

Lan knew they were talking about him.

Hiroki knew they were talking about him.

'I suppose you think you're the next Shane Warne,' Izram said hotly.

'At least I'm the right colour,' said the second blond.

Lan glanced at the coach who was standing nearby. Why didn't he say something? 'Okay everyone, pad up!' the coach called. 'Let's see your form in the nets.'

Lan put his arm around Izram. 'Don't worry about those shits, Iz. We'll show them in the nets.'

They didn't, of course. The three blonds performed as if they'd been born gripping a cricket bat. Lan and most of the other North Illaba hopefuls performed as if a cricket bat was something they'd found lying on the side of the road and were wondering what it was used for.

Lan had only been in the nets a few minutes when his time was up. 'You're lifting the ball!' the coach yelled. 'Next!'

What did he mean, lifting the ball? Was that bad? Lan handed the bat to the next boy and trudged off. Even in that short time he had loved the way the bat had felt in his hand. He had even enjoyed facing up to the balls, scary though it had been.

'You did okay,' Izram said, helping him off with his pads.

'Yeah, not bad,' Andy agreed.

Lan knew they were being generous. He had been pathetic. Just as he'd been pathetic at slips catching and fielding and wicket-keeping. As for bowling, forget it. He'd never be a bowler. And he'd never be a batsman either, apparently. That didn't leave much scope.

Through it all the men with clipboards watched and talked among themselves and scribbled notes.

'What do you reckon they're writing about us?' Lan asked.

'Nothin' good,' Andy replied.

'Well, what do they expect? Hardly any of us have played before. Should we tell them that?'

Izram said, 'I think they might know by now.'

The Chinese boy was batting in the nets. He'd been there much longer than two minutes, Lan calculated. The coach wasn't calling 'Out!' to him. Lan wondered again who he was.

'He's a good hard slogger,' Andy said. 'Wish he was in our team.'

Lan tried not to feel down-hearted. Okay, his players hadn't performed so brilliantly but he hadn't expected them to, had he? And there were a number of things to be pleased about. Over half of those who had attended the Thursday meeting at school had turned up; Tomas was so keen he'd even brought an interpreter. Some could actually catch and whack a ball (even if he wasn't one of them), and Mr Burridge knew about them now and would help them select and organise their team.

It had been a worthwhile morning, he reckoned.

The session finished a little before twelve. After the equipment had been collected and packed away the chairman of selectors gathered everyone together. 'We've seen some real talent here this morning, lads,' he began.

'And some real wastes of space,' Macca murmured.

The Chinese boy, who happened to be standing next to him, suddenly thrust his bat downwards. Perhaps he hadn't noticed the blond's foot was there. Perhaps he was tired and just wanted to lean on his bat for awhile. In any case, it landed square and heavy on Macca's instep. He yelped with pain.

'Sorry.' The Chinese boy's face was blank.

Good one, Lan thought gleefully. Who *was* this guy?

The chairman was still speaking. '. . . and in about a week or so we'll write and let you know if you've been selected. As I said, we're only fielding two junior teams this season, a Green and a Gold, so I'm afraid a lot of you are going to miss out. But good luck and thanks again for coming.'

The crowd broke up. The fathers waiting on the edges of the oval stirred themselves. Car engines started.

'Guess we won't be seeing you Nips again,' Second Blond said. He and his friends sauntered off.

'What a bunch of jerks,' Izram said.

'Forget about them,' Lan said. 'What did that chairman mean, only two teams? What about our team?' Just register with the club and you'll be able to play, Mr Hussein had said. That might be how it worked in Lahore but it seemed to be totally different here.

He looked around for Mr Burridge. The secretary, the selectors and the coach were talking together near the entrance to the club bar which had just opened. They were consulting clipboards. Papers were being passed around.

'Will they give us some gear?' Hiroki asked.

'What do we do if they don't?' Andy asked.

'I think we should speak to that Mr Burridge,' Lan said.

'Better hurry,' said Andy. 'Looks like they're going off for a beer.'

'You all wait here,' Lan said. 'Me and Iz will go.' The two boys ran up. Lan said, 'Excuse me, Mr Burridge, can we talk to you about our team?'

Mr Burridge turned around. He had indeed been heading towards a nice cold beer with the chairman. 'Ah!' he said. 'These are the lads I told you about, Barry.'

The chairman and the other men turned. They smiled vaguely at Lan and Izram and then at the others standing at the edge of the oval.

'Good to see you all so interested in cricket,' Barry

the chairman said jovially. 'Haven't played much, I take it?'

'You'll improve with practice,' said one of the selectors in what he hoped was an encouraging way.

'We all have to start somewhere,' said the other.

But not with the Illaba Cricket Club, their expressions said plainly.

'We didn't get picked, did we?' Lan asked.

'We haven't made our selections yet, son,' the chairman said.

'There were a lot of very good players here this morning,' a selector added.

'We don't get many of your lot playing the game,' said the coach.

'Your lot' was just another way of saying 'Nips', Lan thought. It occurred to him that by forming their own cricket team they'd be taking a little bit of power into their own hands. They wouldn't have to rely on selectors or people like the coach who probably thought that to play cricket well one had to be Anglo. And they wouldn't have to play with arrogant jerks like the three blonds. 'As a matter of fact, we don't want to play for the Greens and Golds,' he said.

The chairman looked indignant. He opened his mouth to speak and Lan, remembering the equipment they still didn't have, went on quickly: 'They're probably terrific teams and all that but we've got our own team. We just want help in getting it organised.'

'Organised?' queried the chairman.

'Yeah. Mr Burridge said —'

Mr Burridge gave a little cough. 'Why don't I have a word with the lads and sort this out?' he suggested. 'I'll see you later in the bar, shall I?'

This seemed to suit everyone.

'Come into my office,' Mr Burridge said to Lan and Izram. 'Just you two, I think. It's rather a small office.'

It *was* a small office. By the time all three of them were seated, there wasn't enough room to swing a cricket bat, as Mr Burridge cheerfully observed. 'Still, that's not what we're here for, is it? Now, Lan, is it? And you are — ?'

'Izram Hussein.'

'And you're from where? Which school?'

'North Illaba Primary,' Lan said.

'Right. That's what I meant, by the way, when I asked you that question at registration. Now, how about telling me about this team of yours?' He leaned back in his chair and laced his fingers across his stomach.

Perhaps Mr Burridge wasn't so bad after all, Lan thought. He explained all about his Big Idea and Mr Drummond giving them a week and Mr Hussein telling them how it was done in Lahore. He didn't mention a match against King's. After this morning's session, Mr Burridge would probably split his sides laughing.

'So now we've got all these people who want to play cricket —'

'And we need equipment and somewhere to practise and someone to coach us,' Izram finished.

'Someone who doesn't think cricket's a game for Anglos only,' Lan added.

Mr Burridge looked a little embarrassed. 'Ah, that's just the coach. You don't want to take any notice of him.' He sat up straight and shuffled his papers.

'First off, you have to understand that club cricket's different from school cricket. Anybody can play school cricket. Everybody gets a go, no matter what kind of player they are. But club cricket's a step up from that. It's more organised and we're looking for good players, players with potential. It's not the right environment for young rookies like you and your mates. But your school's not a goer either, eh? Let's have a think.'

Lan and Izram waited.

'Well, first off, there's nothing to stop you playing on the Denby Street reserve. Just round the corner from here, you know it? There's nets there and that's what beginners need, a lot of practice in the nets. Just clear off by the time the teams start their practice.'

'We don't have any equipment,' Lan said.

'Nothing at all? No bats, gloves, pads? A couple of balls?'

Lan and Izram shook their heads.

'We thought we might be able to borrow stuff from the club,' Izram said.

'Well, you're not members, see. That's the problem.'

'Does that cost money?' Lan asked.

'Well, yes.' Mr Burridge remembered the kid who didn't speak English. Perhaps these were refugee kids. 'Look, leave it with me,' he said. 'I'll make some inquiries and see what I can rustle up. In the meantime, start practising with any old thing that comes to hand. You know how the great Don Bradman used to practise?'

As it happened, Lan did. He'd seen it on the video he'd borrowed from the library. 'He hit a golf ball against a tank stand with an old cricket stump.'

Mr Burridge looked surprised. 'That's right, he did. In his backyard, over and over again, for hours at a time, day after day. The great Richie Benaud used to practise by bowling at a handkerchief. So you don't need a lot of equipment to begin with, although you'll want your own bat eventually. But if you're serious about playing you're going to need some coaching. And that costs money.'

His mother had been right, Lan thought. All sports ended up costing money. 'How much?'

'Well, it varies. But as a sort of guide, a group coaching clinic would cost you around $10 an hour. Say six in a group, so an accredited coach is looking for about $60 an hour. You'll be lucky if you find one to take on a team for that, though. Individual coaching costs much more, of course.'

He saw their faces. 'Out of the question, eh? What about one of your teachers?'

'We could try,' Lan said doubtfully. They didn't have many male teachers at North Illaba. How many — five? Two were practically old-age pensioners and Mr Scutter had one arm.

'What about one of your dads then? That's usually the way it works at your age.'

'I don't think any of us have dads who play cricket,' Lan said. Then he brightened. 'Except Mr Hussein. That's Iz's dad. He said every Pakistani could play cricket, didn't he, Iz? Reckon he'd coach us?'

Izram said he would ask.

Mr Burridge rubbed his hands together and stood up. 'That's the ticket! Get your families involved. Cricket ought to be a family game. Well, it looks like we're on our way. You give me a ring about the middle of next week — there's my card — and I'll see what I can do for you.'

'Thanks, Mr Burridge.'

'Call me Burrie, everyone here does.'

'Thanks, Mr Burrie.'

The club secretary walked to the entrance with them and watched them dash off to join their mates. They were nice kids. He liked to see nice kids playing cricket. None of them had shown much potential this morning but they were young, they were trying hard and they were genuine. He'd do his best for them.

'Just for the record,' he called, 'what's the name of your team?'

Lan turned around. 'The Nips,' he called back.

Mr Burridge managed a weak smile.

'*What* did you say our team was called?' Hiroki asked. 'Did you say *Nips*? My parents will freak!'

'We're only calling ourselves what they call us,' Andy Chen said.

'I like it,' said Phon. 'It's sort of a joke, yes?'

'Drummo won't see the joke. He'll crack a fruity!'

'I'm not a Nip,' Sal Catano objected.

'No, you're a wog, you wog!'

'So what's Iz? A Nip or a wog?'

'A Paki.'

'And Akka? And him?' He pointed at Tomas.

'I'm the Nip,' Lan said loudly, before things got out of hand. 'This team is all my idea so I get to name it. That's how you name cricket teams, in case you don't know. Like the Prime Minister's XI. Not everyone in the team's a prime minister, are they?'

Hiroki still looked worried. 'But it's what foreigners call Asians. Those blond guys used it, I heard them. We shouldn't use the word too.'

'Why not?' Andy asked. 'It shows we don't care.'

'I think it's a good name.'

Lan looked around to see who was speaking. It was the Chinese boy with the lethal cricket bat. Why was he still here?

Andy said, 'Lan, this is David Ho. I told him about us and he wants to join our team.'

'Why?' Lan asked in surprise. 'I mean, you were pretty good this morning. You might get selected for the Greens or the Golds.'

David shrugged. 'Maybe, maybe not. I'd still like to play with you.'

Izram whispered, 'We need at least one good batsman. And he's got a bat.'

Lan remembered how David had used it. In the nets and on those toes. How could he turn down someone like that? 'We haven't really got a team yet,' he said honestly, 'and some of us are real beginners.' Well, he'd know that by now. 'And we'll be doing a lot of training, once we find a coach.'

'That's okay,' said David. 'Does it matter that I don't go to your school?'

Lan shook his head. 'Not when you're a Nip.'

They grinned at each other. David was in.

'So what's happening?' Andy asked. 'What did the guy from the cricket club say?'

'Oh yeah.' Lan told them the news. 'Izzie's going to ask his dad to coach us. That is, unless anyone else has a dad who plays cricket?'

Nobody had.

Lan decided he ought to say a few words of encouragement. If he wasn't the captain — there wasn't yet a team to be captain of — he was at least the team manager. And someone had to motivate and encourage the players.

'You all did great this morning,' he began, 'especially the beginners.' He saw a few doubting faces. 'Don't measure yourselves against the others who were here. Mr Burrie said they were the best players from all the schools in the district. We're just starting off. All we need is a coach and the proper gear and I reckon we'll soon be playing as good as them. Better!'

They all cheered.

Lan remembered Tomas. 'Hey, Tom? Onya!' He gave him the thumbs up.

'Onya!' said Tomas. Beaming, he returned the gesture.

Lan thanked them again for coming. 'See you on Monday then.'

'See ya!'

They drifted off looking very motivated.

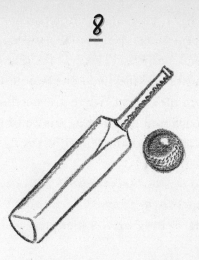

8

Izram felt hot and sweaty. As soon as he was out of sight of the oval he took off his tracksuit top. Whew! That was better. Next time he'd wear a baggy T-shirt, not one of these tank tops that showed up all your rolls of fat. And when he was playing real cricket — *if* he got to play — he'd wear a shirt and long white pants, like a Test cricketer. That was one good thing about cricket: you didn't play in shorts and singlet.

On a school report a year or so ago his physical education teacher had written: 'Izram has no inclination to move whatsoever.' It wasn't true: Izram wanted very much to run about and play ball games but when he did his fat wobbled. And because of the shorts and singlet that were compulsory for PE everyone could see it wobbling.

Curry Guts, somebody had called him.

He'd given up sport and the school had shortly afterwards given up physical education. The funding had been cut and the teacher had left. But now he was in the Nips, would he have to train in shorts and singlet?

Not if his dad was coach, he thought with relief. He'd let him wear whatever he liked.

Akram had worn all the wrong stuff, as usual. The trouble was, when he looked at himself at home he looked okay. When he got with others he knew he was a loser.

Today, for instance. His T-shirt had stripes. Mistake. Nobody over five wore stripes, he knew that now. His mother had made him wear a singlet under it and it had been plainly visible whenever he'd raised his arms. Even bigger mistake. His trainers didn't have a red star on the side (mistake), his track pants were blue instead of black or grey (mistake) and the Snoopy socks probably hadn't been a good idea.

Those blond guys had looked cool. They were total jerks, of course, but Akram had noticed that people who wore all the right gear often were. Or per-haps they just behaved that way to people like him who didn't.

Akram longed to be trendy, to be one of the group who wore the right clothes as if they'd been born to them. He'd see people around school and in the mall wearing new and different clothes and then he'd notice more people wearing similar clothes and he'd work out that this was the latest fashion. But how did *they* know, and so far in advance? By the time he'd got round to deciding whether he liked something — cargo pants, for instance — they'd be on their way out or, even worse, so far behind that just wearing them marked you out right away as a nerd. Even when he managed to wear something while it was still reasonably trendy, it somehow didn't look as good on him as on everyone else. Perhaps it was something to do with being an Arab.

Arabs didn't play cricket, his father said. Arabs didn't look like those blond guys either. There was a difference between wogs and Anglos. Some of it was to do with the games they played and some of it was to do with what they wore and how they looked.

If he'd been wearing the right gear today, he would have played a lot better. Anyway, how could you bat or field properly when you were too worried about your singlet to raise your arms?

Tomas thought it had been the best morning since he'd come to this country, a country he thought he would never feel right in.

From his first day he'd hated the school. Everyone in it looked different, they learnt different things and ate different food and he couldn't understand what they were saying half the time. No, *most* of the time. The language was supposed to be English but it wasn't much like the English he'd learnt during his weeks at the hostel. Nobody here spoke Spanish. He was worse than a baby, he was a mute.

Every morning he begged to stay at home. His mother had been a teacher in El Salvador, she could teach him. But she said no. She had to learn English, too, and find a job. Besides, it was important to mix with Australian children. But that was just it. He didn't. How could you mix when you were different and couldn't speak the language?

His father had lost a job because he couldn't understand English. They'd told him to come on Tuesday and he had understood Thursday. When he turned up, they told him they'd given the job to someone else. He'd come home with tears in his eyes. Then his mother had cried, because it was his first job and they needed the money.

'It will get easier,' his mother kept saying. 'You'll get used to things.'

She was partly right. He'd gradually got used to the school routine. He got used to spending recess alone. Occasionally he joined in kicking a ball around, but then the game stopped and people started talking and he'd wander off. He got used to not laughing because he never understood the jokes. He got used to walking home alone. He got used to words flying around in his head, only occasionally forming themselves into sentences he could understand. It was possible to get used to most things, however horrible they were.

But it didn't get easier. Each night he'd go to bed praying that next morning he wouldn't have to get up and go to school. He wasn't sure what would be necessary to bring this about. A war or a revolution perhaps, but it seemed stupid to pray for that when you'd just escaped from one. A fire that burned down the entire school? They'd only send him to another school and that would be just as bad. Worse, in fact, because he'd have to start from the very beginning, and if you rated Getting-Used-To-Things on a scale of one to ten he'd at least passed one.

He'd zoomed up the scale now. He might easily be as high as six! And all because of cricket.

Lan had said he didn't want to be different and Tomas had understood perfectly. He hated being different, too. If playing cricket would make him more Australian, he wanted to play it.

His mother had been pleased. A son playing cricket was better than a son thinking about burning down the school. She'd told her friend Maria and as a result Maria's son, Paolo, who spoke English, had come with him this morning. Just in case there were forms to fill out, or important things he had to understand.

He had hit the ball. Twice! He had learnt how to take wickets. He was in a team where others had skin as dark as or darker than his own. He had learnt a new word: Onya!

He was a Nip.

Andy waited at the bus-stop. The question was: did he want to play cricket or not?

He'd never made the grade back in Malaysia and he'd been pretty hopeless this morning too, no matter what Lan had said. Not that Lan would know anything about it.

Did he actually *like* cricket? Andy wasn't sure.

He rather liked the idea of being one of those people who stayed indoors on a summer weekend, watching a Test match on TV that half the country seemed to be watching too. In his mind's eye he saw himself at school on Monday morning, shaking his head in admiration: 'Jeez, what about that Warnie, hey? Whatta legend!'

He liked the idea of being able to say casually, 'Sorry, I can't come round on Saturday, I'm playing cricket.'

He liked the idea of carrying a bag full of cricket gear onto the bus and all the girls thinking he was a true-blue sportsman.

But was his heart really in it? And if it wasn't, could he go the distance? While he was playing or watching cricket he could understand why he was doing it, but when he wasn't he couldn't quite summon up the necessary energy.

Except that it was one way of being less Chinese.

Lan and David sat on the grass under a tree and waited for David's father to arrive. David had rung him to say the session had finished and he was ready to be picked up.

Wow, thought Lan: two people on the team with mobiles!

David went to Hamilton College. 'That's a rich school, isn't it?' Lan said.

David shrugged.

'Bet they don't call you Nip there.'

'They called me something else when I first started.'

'Yeah? What?'

'Hong Kong Stir-Fry. My first day there and they gave me that nickname. Because of all those TV ads for that crap sauce in a jar. I came home and told my parents I had to change schools. My dad just made a joke of it.'

'They still call you Stir-Fry?'

'Sometimes. I don't care any more. Everyone eats stir-fry so how is it an insult? They used to call Italians spags. You know, for spaghetti. But everyone eats the stuff now, so what's the point? Once they knew I didn't care, they stopped.'

'Yeah. But spags — wogs, you know, Greeks and Italians, like Sal, they have it easier, though, I reckon. They don't look all that different from Australians. But we're all Asians. Even if we're born here, we're Asians. When we're wrinklies in wheelchairs we'll still be Asians.'

'Rice boys.'

'Chinks.'

'Nips.'

'Yeah. Nips.'

'Is that what this cricket thing's about?' David asked. 'It's not just getting out of lion dancing and all that multicultural stuff, is it?'

'That's part of it. Don't you ever get fed up? All these Multiculti Days do is stick us all in our little ethnic slots. Well, bugger them!'

David burst out laughing. 'Bugger them! How about that for our team slogan?' He laughed again.

Lan grinned. 'I can just see it on our caps: *Bugger Them*.'

9

Lan's good mood lasted all the way home. It lasted all through the afternoon as he stacked shelves and checked the stock and wrapped groceries in his father's shop.

It lasted until Izram rang that evening to say his father wasn't enthusiastic about being their coach.

'He says he's too busy with the restaurant. He says he hasn't played cricket for years. He says we should get someone else to coach us.'

'Who?' Lan said despondently. ' I can't think of anyone, can you?'

Izram couldn't.

'I guess we could put an ad in the paper, ' Lan said. 'In the Jobs Vacant or something.'

'That sounds as if we're paying a salary,' Izram objected. 'We want someone who'll coach us for free. I don't think we ought to put it under jobs.'

'Where then? Have you got a paper? Can you take a look?'

'Hang on.'

Izram was away for a long time. When he came back he said, 'There's a page called *Personals*. It says *For people wishing to establish contact with others* and there's a phone number.'

'That's us. Are there any coaches?'

'Um ... a couple of ads looking for teachers. Lots of *professional* people. Everyone says they're slim and attractive and easygoing.'

'It doesn't matter what the coach looks like,' Lan said.

'Easygoing would be good, though.'

'Not in a cricket coach. What else do the ads say? Wait a sec, I'll get a pen ... Okay, read some out.'

'Um ... *Fun-loving lady seeks cute spunky gent who has time on his hands* ... Don't they talk funny in these ads? *Youthful and fit* ... We should ask for that. *Likes having a good time* ... *non-smoker* — that's important, otherwise Drummo won't let him near the school ... *fun-loving professional in good health wishes to meet a sensitive gent* ... *likes wining and dining, movies, walks on the beach* ... *Must be genuine.*'

'That sounds good. We should put that.'

'What? About the movies and walks on the beach?'

'No, you dicko. The genuine bit. "Must be a genuine cricket coach."'

'Except that if he is, he'll want to be paid, like Mr Burrie said. We want someone who knows about cricket and who'll coach us for free. And put that we're only kids.'

'Well, how about something like this?' Lan looked at the words he'd scribbled down. *"Young cricketers seek fun-loving gent who knows all about the game and has time on his hands and will do it for free. Must be fit and healthy and a non-smoker."'*

'That sounds all right. And then you put a phone number.'

'We'd better put yours. My mum doesn't like answering the phone. She'll freak out if a lot of men start ringing.'

So would his mum, Izram reflected. 'How many words is that? It costs $8.50 for two lines.'

'How many words in a line?'

'Hang on.' There was silence, then Izram said, 'It's hard to work out. Are words with hyphens like fun-loving and warm-blooded one or two words? Anyway, I reckon it's about four lines. Maybe five.'

'Jeez!' Lan didn't have the money. He knew Izram didn't either. How else could they advertise for a coach?

Lan suddenly remembered the community notices in the library. It had been covered with ads: people looking for or seeking work as babysitters, gardeners, house painters ...

I've got an idea.' He told Izram about the notice-board. 'I'll make a big notice with coloured Textas so it'll stand out. And it won't cost us anything. We'll go after school on Monday and put it up next to the cricket-club stuff. I bet we get someone right away.'

'You have good ideas,' Izram said admiringly.

Their notice was sure to stand out, Lan and Izram agreed. Lan had used the full range of his coloured Textas and had decorated it with pictures of cricket bats clipped from a sports store catalogue. (Forty-five dollars for a junior bat!) He had drawn stars and a green and gold border around the heading:

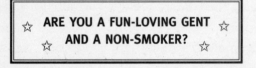

☆ **ARE YOU A FUN-LOVING GENT** ☆
☆ **AND A NON-SMOKER?** ☆

At the bottom he had stuck a picture of Mark Taylor, Cricket Legend.

'Why's he only got half an arm?' Izram asked.

'It's from an ad. I had to cut out the air conditioner. It looks okay though, doesn't it?' Lan said.

'It's great. Where are we going to stick it?'

Izram had a point.

It was hard to believe that there were so many things to do. The community noticeboard in the library was chock-a-block with announcements of pending fêtes and frolics, trading tables, craft markets, book and bridge clubs, eco walks, skydiving, weight-control classes, movie mornings and prawn nights. And dozens of plumbers, carpenters, babysitters, lawnmowers, tree fellers and house-cleaners were looking for work.

No cricket coaches, Lan noticed.

'We'll have to stick it over the top of something,' Izram said. 'What about that spotty old one for Grand Master Jim Chong's Wing Chun classes?'

'Good thinking, Iz. And what about when Grand Master Jim comes after us when he finds out what we've done to his notice?'

'Aquarobics for Seniors then.'

While it seemed a safer option, Lan had a feeling it might be against the law to mess around with community noticeboards. He didn't want to risk being thrown out of the library or having his borrower's card confiscated. Not at this early and vital stage of his cricketing career.

'There's a nice librarian here who knows about cricket. Let's go and ask her,' he said.

She was at the front desk, sweeping a laser gun over returned books faster than a supermarket checker. Was she Miss Grace or Mrs Grace or just Grace, Lan wondered.

He said, 'Can I ask you a question about the noticeboard?'

'Of course.' She looked up and smiled. 'Oh, it's the good all-rounder! Is it cricket, again?'

Lan nodded. 'We want to put this up on the noticeboard but there's no room. Can you find us a space, please?' He slid the notice across the desk to her.

Grace put aside her laser gun and read it. The corners of her mouth twitched. 'Is it a cricket coach you're looking for?' she asked.

Wasn't that obvious, Lan thought. Perhaps Grace wasn't as bright as she seemed.

'Someone who knows all about cricket,' he said, 'but who isn't a professional.'

'Because we can't pay him much,' Izram explained.

'We can't pay him anything,' Lan said. It was best to be honest about these things.

He told Grace about the Nips. She looked thoughtful. 'You know, I think I might have a coach for you.'

Their eyebrows shot up and Lan gave Izram a nudge which meant 'See, I told you she knew about cricket'.

'He might not agree, of course,' Grace said. 'It's quite a while since he's played, but he *did* play for Australia.'

They gaped at her.

'A Test cricketer?'

'Here? In Illaba?'

'Right here in this library as we speak,' Grace said. 'He comes in most days.'

Their heads swivelled as their eyes scanned the library — or the parts of it they could see from the front desk. Who was it?

Lan's gaze settled on a tall man in sweat pants and trainers who stood casually spinning the video display racks. He had fine broad shoulders and his gleaming fair hair was swept back from his forehead. His eyes squinted a little, as if he were sizing up a distant batsman. You could tell from the casual flick of his wrist that he was a bowler. Probably a leggie.

'It's him, isn't it?'

Grace shook her head.

'Then I reckon it's him.' Izram's choice stood at the Returns counter, looking smart yet athletic in his dark blue jacket and well-pressed grey trousers. He bounced lightly on his heels as he peered at the cover of *Sports Illustrated* and tapped a rolled umbrella against his right leg. Just like a batsman waiting at the non-striker's end, Izram thought.

Grace shook her head again. 'I'm afraid you don't … Well, I'd better explain. Have you ever heard of Clarence McGinty? No, you're too young, of course. It was nearly fifty years ago. Most people around here have forgotten him. You have to be a real cricket buff to recall the name. But in his day, believe me, he was one of the most famous names in Australian cricket. And do you know why?'

How would they, Lan thought, if they'd never even heard of Clarence McGinty? But it was one of those questions that didn't require an answer apparently, because the librarian immediately told them.

'He was a mystery spinner!'

Lan frowned. 'Nobody knew who he was?'

'She means nobody knew how he made the ball spin,' Izram said.

'You're both right. When he came along nobody in cricket had even heard of Clarrie McGinty. He hadn't played for his school first XI, he didn't play district or club cricket. And he was well into his twenties when one day he wandered down to the Illaba Oval and asked if he could play a game. They put him in the third XI, their bottom team. Within three years he was playing for the state and then he was picked for Australia. And it was all because of his bowling.'

Grace held her hand out towards them, palm up.

'He had this unusual method. The middle finger was doubled back under the ball, like this. Oooh!' She grimaced. 'I can't do it very well.'

'Like this?' Lan demonstrated.

'That's it. You have to have long flexible fingers, like Clarrie. He'd practised this technique for years, apparently, using a ping-pong ball. He was very strong, with big hands, and he delivered it with a sharp off-spin and batsmen just couldn't cope. It didn't matter that he couldn't bat or field. His bowling was so extraordinary he was picked to play for Australia. And according to most of the experts, it was Clarrie's bowling that won the Ashes for Australia that season.'

'Wow!' So it *was* possible, Lan thought. You could come from nowhere, with hardly any cricket experience, and still stun the world.

'What happened to him?' asked Izram.

'It was quite sad, really,' Grace said. 'He had a very brief career. His wife died while he was away playing cricket, and some people thought that was the reason he gave up. You know, that he blamed the game. He certainly never played again. He dropped out and after a while most people forgot about him. I don't think he even watches the club games these days. Most people around here don't know who he is.'

'How do you know about him?' Lan asked.

'Through our history museum. I helped them computerise their records a few years ago, and I read all about Spinner. That was his nickname: Spinner McGinty. And I thought to myself, my goodness, that's the old chap who comes into the library every afternoon.'

'And he's in here now?'

Their eyes were everywhere, even as they listened to her.

'He is. But boys ...' Grace hesitated. 'He's not young any more and he's lived on his own for a long time. He doesn't have anyone at home to look after him. You have to keep that in mind. And he can be a bit grumpy. Shall I take you over, and then you can ask him about the coaching?'

'Yes, please.'

Lan and Izram exchanged excited glances. A real Test cricketer! The Nips would go bananas. Well, those who could tell a Warnie from a Waugh would.

The librarian lifted a portion of the desk and came out from behind it. 'Come with me.'

They followed her past New Books and General Fiction and into the side section of the library where the newspapers and magazines were displayed on racks. Long windows on the west wall let in the afternoon sun, and comfortable chairs encouraged readers to linger. A few were occupied now. Lan eyed an elderly gentleman who looked rather grumpy but Grace went straight past him.

She seemed to be heading for the computer room at the rear of the library. The mystery spinner must spend a lot of time on the Internet, Lan decided. There were lots of cool cricket sites.

Izram thought otherwise. He nudged Lan and whispered, 'Bet she pays out that old dero sitting by the window.'

The old man seemed to be asleep. Although there was a folded newspaper on his lap, his chin was resting on his chest and his eyes were closed. His clothes were shabby and crumpled, as if he'd been sleeping in them for a week. Perhaps he had, Lan thought. He hoped Grace wasn't going to throw him out. Perhaps he didn't have a home to go to. It was certainly nicer sleeping in a comfortable library chair than on a park bench or one of those hard plastic seats in the shopping mall.

Izram nudged him again. 'He's got a dog.'

Lan hadn't noticed the dog, but now his gaze dropped to the floor. Lying next to the old man's feet in their scuffed, down-at-heel brown shoes was a small black and white fox terrier. Like his master, he appeared to be asleep, but his head lifted and his ears pricked up as Grace approached.

Lan felt indignant. There were plenty of chairs in the library. The old bloke was sleeping and not disturbing anyone. The little dog was so quiet he hadn't even noticed him. True, neither of them was reading but it must be good for the soul just to sleep surrounded by Great Literature.

Better than being surrounded by a supermarket and the Quicka Liqua store, anyway.

Grace marched up to them.

She wasn't so nice after all, Lan reflected.

Grace touched the old man gently on the shoulder.

'Spinner,' she said, 'there's a couple of young cricketers I'd like you to meet.'

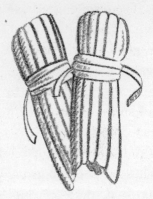

10

Perhaps he hadn't been asleep after all, because his eyes opened right away. Grace repeated her introduction.

'I heard ya the first time,' he grumbled. 'I'm not deaf yet.' His eyes swivelled towards the boys. 'Friends of yours are they, WG?'

Grace nudged them forward. 'This is Lan, and this is —' She paused because of course she didn't know.

'Izram. Izram Hussein.'

His voice sounded quite normal. Lan shot him a glance. Didn't Iz feel as surprised and shocked as he did? He couldn't believe that this old dero was an ex-Test cricketer who'd worn the baggy green cap. He looked as if the closest he'd ever come to the Ashes was rooting about in a dustbin.

'Good cricketers, the Pakis,' McGinty said. 'Good cooks, too.'

Izram beamed.

He looked at Lan. 'You a good cricketer, too?'

His eyes were round and hazel and more alert than Lan had expected them to be. 'I'm working on it,' he said.

'That's the only way.'

'Do you think Asians make good cricketers?' Lan asked.

'Some of 'em. Sri Lankans, Indians, Pakis, they're all better than the Poms these days.' The old man cackled, revealing a row of teeth like a crooked picket fence. When the cackle turned into a rasping cough, he put the newspaper aside and pulled a grubby handker- chief from his pocket.

Lan waited until he'd recovered and then said, 'I'm Vietnamese.'

'Don't think they play cricket, do they?' McGinty said, stuffing the handkerchief back into the depths of his baggy trousers.

'Not in Vietnam. But we should play if we're liv- ing in Australia, don't you think?'

The old man squinted up at Grace. 'What's this all about, WG?'

'The boys and their friends are looking for a cricket coach. Their school doesn't play and neither do their parents. They were going to put up a notice in the library, but then I remembered you sitting here most days with nothing to do but read the papers.'

McGinty snorted. 'Get out of it! Do I look like I could coach a pack of kids?'

No, he didn't, Lan thought. But Grace said, 'I don't see why not. It would give you an interest—'

'Bugger that.'

'And it would be good for the boys. Didn't you tell me just the other day that kids should be out on the oval playing ball games instead of inside a library playing on computers?'

'Never said I'd take 'em out and teach 'em,' McGinty grumbled.

'Well, how else are they going to learn?' Grace asked reasonably, as if he, Clarence McGinty, was absolutely the only cricket coach in the district. 'I'll let them tell you all about it. I'm afraid I've got to get back to the front desk.'

'Show Spinner your advertisement,' she said to Lan, before departing.

Lan wasn't sure that was such a good idea. This old man clearly didn't fit the job description. He wasn't fit, he didn't look at all healthy, and judging by the yellow stains on his fingers, he was a smoker. Anyone who sat around the library all day couldn't be described as fun-loving. He might not even be a gent.

'Give us a look.' McGinty gestured towards the notice.

With a sidelong glance at Izram, Lan handed it over.

'Where's me specs?' McGinty reached in the top pocket of his shirt which Lan noticed had an egg stain down its front. He pulled out a pair, the frames heavily repaired with brown tape, and put them on.

'Now then, what've we got here? Why don't you two take the weight off yer pins while I'm readin' this impressive-lookin' document.'

What weight? What pins? Lan and Izram didn't move.

'Take a chair, siddown!'

Lan and Izram pulled up a couple of chairs and sat down. The fox terrier wagged its tail and looked at them in a friendly way.

McGinty read the notice in silence.

Lan wondered whether he should explain why Mark Taylor had only half an arm.

He decided it was unlikely to be the deciding factor.

'Sounds like a highly desirable appointment,' McGinty said at last, taking off his glasses. 'Every old player in the country will be queuing up for this once word gets around.'

Lan was surprised. Was his ad *that* good?

'You won't get Greg Chappell, of course. The Redbacks have nabbed 'im. But if I see Lillee or Thommo on me travels, I'll let 'em know there's an opening.'

'Thanks, Mr McGinty,' Lan said. 'That'd be great. But it'll have to be quick. We're playing a match at the end of the year. In front of the whole school. So we need to start right away.'

McGinty looked at him for a long moment. 'Are they all like you in the team?' he asked.

'A few of them. Some are Chinese. Hiroki's Japanese. There's a couple of Cambodians. Phon's from Thailand, Satto's from Indonesia ...'

'Gawd! A regular United Nations. How long you been playin' cricket?'

'Not long,' Lan said.

'Three days,' Izram said.

McGinty's expression didn't alter. 'And at the end of the year you're playin' a big exhibition match?'

'That's why we need a lot of coaching,' Lan explained.

'I'm with yer there. What about gear? Bats, pads, balls and all the rest of it?'

Izram shook his head. 'We haven't got anything yet. Well, David's got a bat.'

'Grace told us you used to practise with a ping-pong ball,' Lan said.

'I did. But I didn't try to play a match with one.' He stroked his stubbly chin thoughtfully. His hands were huge, Lan noticed. 'Y'know what you blokes oughta do? Go and see the Illaba Cricket Club. They've got players and coaches comin' outta their ears. They'll get you started, no worries.'

'We did go and see them,' Lan said, 'but we weren't good enough to play in their teams.'

'And you have to be a member to use their gear,' Izram added.

'They're gettin' a bit elitist,' McGinty said. 'Boys, I wish I could help you but me cricketin' days are long over. I don't reckon I've even picked up a bat in the last thirty years or more. Not that I was ever any great shakes as a batsman. You need some young bloke, not an old crock like me.'

'I think you're right,' Lan said.

Izram threw him a startled glance.

'It was Grace's idea, but it wasn't fair to ask you,' Lan said. 'Old people need lots of rest and quiet. That's a bad cough you've got, Mr McGinty, and you don't see very well either. I guess your legs are a bit wobbly, too.'

'I s'pose you think me brain's a bit wobbly as well?' McGinty growled.

'Old people forget things,' Lan said, trying to be kind.

'It's called Old Timers' Disease,' Izram added helpfully.

'Strewth, listen to 'em! Me eyesight's gone and me hearing's shot to bits! I knew I shoulda become an umpire. You're being a bit bloody picky for a team that can't pay a coach a brass razoo.'

Izram said, 'Um, I think I need a word with my team-mate.'

He pulled Lan out of sight behind the CD racks.

'Now you've made him cross. Telling him he's clapped out and past it! He'll never coach us now.'

'Do we really want him to? Iz, look at him!'

'Who else have we got?'

'We'll find someone. I'll put the notice up.'

'It might take weeks. And he's right. Nobody who's any good will coach us for free. We haven't got any money, so how else can we pay him? I wonder if there's anything he needs?'

Lan peered through the CDs. 'He needs a wash and a shave and a haircut and new shoes and shirt and trousers and a new pair of glasses. Probably new under-daks, too. He's pretty skinny. Look at how baggy his trousers are. He's using an old tie to hold them up. I bet he doesn't get enough to eat.'

Izram grabbed his arm. 'That's it! Remember what he said about Pakis being good cooks? I bet he loves curries and stuff. We could give him free meals at the Bukhara in exchange for coaching us.'

'Would your dad mind?'

'He's feeling pretty guilty about being too busy to coach us. This way he'll be able to help without actu-ally doing anything. And how much can an old skinny guy like McGinty eat anyway? Let's ask him.'

They returned and resumed their seats.

McGinty looked at their faces and said, 'I take it the management has reached an executive decision?'

'We'd like to offer you the position,' Lan said. 'This is the deal: you coach the team and in exchange you can eat free at the best Indian restaurant in Illaba.'

'*North* Indian,' Izram corrected. 'It's called the Bukhara. My dad owns it. Last year the *Illaba Messenger* gave it eight out of ten for food and six out of ten for ambience. But we've installed a tropical fish tank since then.'

'It's in Mawson Street, just round the corner from the mall,' Lan said.

'I know where it is,' McGinty said.

'Tell him some of the house specials, Iz.'

'Um, Murgh Mussallam, that's chicken baked in yoghurt and served with poppadums; the lamb curry and kebabs are pretty good. Tandoori, of course, and rojan gosht; chicken biryani, vindaloo ...'

McGinty licked his lips. 'I'm partial to a nice hot vindaloo.'

'You can coach us after school and then go straight to the Bukhara and eat anything you want for free,' Lan said. 'Or you can have takeaway.'

'How often would you want coachin' then?'

'Oh, every day, I reckon.'

Izram dug him in the ribs.

'Well, perhaps not *every* day,' Lan amended. 'But we're playing King's College and we've got a lot to learn.'

'King's College, eh? They any good these days?'

'They're the champions. They've been playing cricket for about a hundred years.'

'You don't say. Doesn't mean they can't be beat.' McGinty stroked his chin and seemed lost in thought. At last he said, 'It's a temptin' offer. But I have to consult my team-mate.'

Who was that? Lan wondered. Grace had said his wife was dead.

'You haven't properly met Larri yet. Larri, say gid-day to the boys.'

The fox terrier at his feet pricked up his ears. He stood up and wagged his tail. McGinty scratched him affectionately on the head. 'Larri. Short for larrikin. They're offerin' us free vindaloo, old sport. Whaddya think?'

Larri looked enthusiastic. He licked the old man's hand.

'Reckon you've got yourselves a coach then.'

'And a team mascot,' Lan said. What an intelligent dog. No wonder Grace allowed him in the library. He crouched down and patted Larri's head. He noticed that McGinty was wearing different coloured socks.

'Right, when do we start?' their new coach said. 'And mateys, you can call me Spinner.'

Lan liked him. Suddenly Spinner's age and appearance didn't matter at all. The old man hadn't raised an eyebrow when Lan had mentioned King's. He even seemed to think they could win.

11

Izram was right. Mr Hussein felt so guilty about not coaching the team himself that after a bit of initial grumbling about what he called Curry for Coaching he put up no objection.

'He's a skinny old man with bad teeth. How much can he eat?' Izram asked.

The answer amazed them both.

Spinner McGinty ate as if there were no tomorrow. It wouldn't be long, Izram calculated, before he ate his way through the entire Bukhara menu. What he couldn't finish, Larri polished off. Not even the hottest vindaloo slowed either of them down. 'Think how much he'd eat with good teeth,' he said, trying to find something his father could be grateful for.

But Mr Hussein didn't mind a bit. He'd consulted the Holy Writ of cricket, *Wisden's Almanack*, found

Clarence McGinty's name, and almost fainted with excitement. If he'd had a red carpet he would have rolled it out. Nobody who had played cricket for his country would ever be unwelcome at the Bukhara. It was an honour to serve such a man. And what stories he told!

Spinner usually ate immediately following the after-school practice, so the restaurant was often empty when he turned up. Mr Hussein would serve him and then pull up a chair and chat.

Although separated by years, kilometres and culture, they had come to cricket in similar ways and they reminisced like a pair of old broadcasting commentators. Both agreed that the street was the best place to learn the game.

'There are no cricket academies in Pakistan,' said Mr Hussein. 'No coaches, very few schools with ovals or cricket pitches. Cricket is played in the streets.'

'Used to be the same here,' Spinner said. 'All the kids in the back lane, a kero tin or rubbish bin for the wicket.'

'You had a wicket? We had to whitewash one on a wall.'

'We'd bash away with a makeshift bat and a tennis ball. Over the fence was a sixer. Hit somebody's roof, that was nine.'

'Tennis balls, yes! Same in Lahore. We used to wrap it in tape to make it swing like mad and fly onto the bat. Many games are at night and the light is not so good, you know, so the ball is like a white blur. If you can hit the ball under those conditions, my goodness, you can hit it anywhere. Even at the Gabba when Shane Warne is bowling, hey!'

He thumped Spinner on the shoulder.

Luckily for Spinner, his mouth was uncharacteristically empty. 'I didn't even see a proper bat till I was sixteen,' he said.

'A proper bat! My goodness, you were fortunate. If we had a bat at all it was held together with twine and tape. We often had to play with a piece of wooden box.'

Izram waited for Spinner to say he was so poor he had only cardboard boxes. But he took another mouthful of vindaloo instead.

'How did you learn to play?' Izram asked his father. 'Did you watch games on TV?'

Mr Hussein hooted. 'TV! There was no TV. Even now in Pakistan few people have TV. And if they do, the power is always being cut. No, I went to matches, I watched as many games as I could. I watched the best players and tried to play like them.'

'Still the best way,' said Spinner. 'A young bloke c'n get all the coachin' in the world but his best bet is to study the top players and imitate them.'

'You are right. This is what many Pakistani players do.'

'And the West Indians. Mind you, their battin' technique can be a bit crook. Like mine, come to think of it.'

'And the bowling is sometimes very crazy.'

'Doesn't stop 'em winnin' matches though.'

'My goodness, no. Cricket is no longer an Englishman's game.'

'Course, there's one type of cricketer these young blokes don't need to imitate,' Spinner said. 'I tell yer, sometimes I want to turn off the telly, all the sledgin' and snarlin' and arguin' with the umpire that goes on. That's not cricket, in my opinion.'

'You're an old-fashioned player, Mr Spinner.'

'Too right I am.'

'I agree. Fair play and good sportsmanship is everything in cricket. Sometimes I wonder what the game is coming to.' Mr Hussein shook his head sorrowfully. 'More vindaloo, Mr Spinner?'

'Thanks, don't mind if I do. And a drop of tea, if there's any goin'.'

It was a good thing the Nips had a coach who knew how to play cricket without the proper cricket gear, Lan and Izram agreed. Mr Burrie had not come good.

'There's a bit of a problem with the club management. You know, you not being financial members or members of a club team. The general feeling is your school ought to be providing the equipment. I did manage to rustle you up a pair of gloves and some old balls.' He'd looked a little embarrassed as he handed them over.

'We found a coach,' Lan said.

'That's the shot. One of the dads come good after all, did he?'

Lan shook his head. 'He's a real Test cricketer. At least he used to be. His name's Clarrie McGinty.'

'Good God!' exclaimed Mr Burridge. 'Old Spinner? I thought he was dead.'

He looked so astonished that Lan felt uneasy. It was bad enough trying to learn cricket with only a glove and a few balls but how would they go with a coach so old he apparently ought to be dead?

It turned out, however, that balls — the catching and throwing of — was exactly what Spinner had in mind for them.

He turned up for the first training session at Denby Street reserve looking very much alive, if not quite the picture of a modern professional coach. He seemed to be wearing exactly the same clothes he'd worn that first day in the library, except now there was a battered old Akubra on his head. The same tie held up the same stained and baggy trousers and his long thin neck sprouted from the same grimy shirt collar like an asparagus. He'd changed his socks though, Lan noted. This pair matched.

Lan explained about the lack of equipment. 'But David's got a bat and we've got these balls and a glove.'

'That'll do for a start,' Spinner said.

They gathered around. Lan felt breathless with excitement. This was it; Nips XI was on their way.

'I can't promise to turn ya into brilliant batters or

bowlers, but I can guarantee to turn you all into good fielders,' Spinner announced, tossing one of the balls about in his hand. 'You're all young and nimble, you oughta have good reflexes. So you can all be good fielders.'

Some of Lan's excitement subsided. All his day-dreams were about being a brilliant batsman or bowler. Preferably both. Being a good fielder didn't seem much of an ambition.

'A lot of matches are won in the field,' Spinner continued. 'Miss a catch and it can cost a hundred runs. Let a four go through and it can lose a match.'

Lan changed his mind. Just the thought of doing either made his tummy flip-flop. Imagine being the fielder who lost the match!

Spinner gave them short catches and high catches. He made them run and pick up and throw. He invented lots of catching games. 'Keep your eyes on the ball!' he'd yell at them. 'Keep yer legs together!' (This was frequently directed at Hiroki, who often looked down to see the ball belting through his wide-apart legs.) 'Catches win matches!'

It wasn't long before that phrase was echoing in Lan's head and he was catching balls in his dreams.

'Always carry around a ball of some sort,' Spinner told them. 'Then you're always ready to throw 'n' catch when you've got a few spare minutes. Throw it to a mate, throw it in the air and catch it, chuck it against a wall and take the return. After a while it'll become second nature. You don't need an oval or pitch or nets: do it in the backyard. Do it in the street. Just do it.'

Lan did it with tennis balls, ping-pong balls and odd pieces of fruit from his father's shop. Small navel oranges were the best. But even the hardest navel tended to splatter in a spectacular way when hurled against the side of the shop.

His father was appalled. 'How can you treat food with such disrespect? An orange was like gold on the refugee boats. People would kill for an orange. Now you throw it on a wall!'

The old waste-not-want-not-refugee-boat argument. Lan had heard it a hundred times. It made no sense. He wasn't on a refugee boat. He was in Australia where an orange cost less than twenty cents. There were dozens of them in the shop.

'If you have nothing to do but throw oranges, come inside and stack shelves,' his father grumbled.

Lan also experimented with Spinner's mystery grip. The middle finger was all-important: it had to be bent back into the palm of your hand and then straightened quickly, like a spring, to propel the ball over the top of your thumb in the direction you wanted it to spin. It helped if you were big and strong with long flexible fingers and you'd put in twenty years of practice with a ping-pong ball.

Batting then. The absence of a proper bat was a nuisance but hadn't the great Don himself practised with a stump? Lan made a bat from the slat of a wooden fruit box and stood for hours in the small courtyard at home, hitting the ball against the garage wall.

The twins thought it was a marvellous game.

Lan made them little fruit-box bats too. The three of them stood in a line and bashed their balls against the wall of the garage.

Bang! Bang! Bang!

'Aiyee!' His mother stuck her head out of the garage door, her eyes wide. 'You want me to think I am back in Saigon!'

'This is how Australians learn to play cricket, Ma!' Lan told her.

'I think this is how Australians drive their mothers mad. Go somewhere else. I'm trying to work.'

'Australian mothers don't work in the garage,' Lan muttered under his breath.

He imagined Mrs Warne in the kitchen, heating meat pies and frying chips to build up Shane's strength, while his dad batted a ball around with him in the spacious backyard.

'Now you know why there aren't any Asians playing cricket for Australia,' Lan told the twins.

12

They had a lot of catching up to do.

'We'll be playing against skips who've been whacking a bat and ball around since they were little kids,' Lan told the Nips. 'So from now until the match, that's what we have to do.'

Every lunchtime they gathered with makeshift bats and balls near a large gum tree on the eastern boundary of the school oval. The tree served as the wicket, while the corrugated-iron fences of the houses restricted the ball's flight. If it was belted into a backyard, someone scaled the fence and retrieved it.

'Okay, behind the tree is caught by the wicket-keeper. I'm batting first.'

'Great bowling, Satto!'

'You're out!'

'It bounced!'

'No way! You can't say that wasn't out!'

'The idea's to keep holding the bat, Akka!'

'Nice catch!'

'Bowled! Bowled ya first ball, Izzie!'

'No, it hit below.'

'Yeah right! Bowl him, Lan.'

'That was a slog!'

'If it hits the tree it's a four!'

'Either way you're out, you idiot!'

'Straight through the gates, Roki! You're out!'

'That one didn't spin at all.'

'Cos you're standing on the off-stump, dicko!'

'Oh great, over the fence! Your turn to get it, Lan. Make it quick.'

'C'mon, Lan! Get a move on!'

'I can't find it!'

The ball seemed to have disappeared completely in the long grass of the backyard. Lan poked and swished around while the complaints from over the fence grew louder. Any moment now, somebody was likely to storm out of the back door and kick up a fuss. Then Drummo would hear about it and that would be the end of lunchtime cricket.

His eye lit on a tree loaded with small green grapefruit. He picked one and hefted it in his hands. Even better than navel oranges. He picked another one and shoved them in his pockets and climbed back over the fence.

'Couldn't find the ball. Try this.'

'Are you kidding?'

'There's only ten minutes to go. C'mon. Bet it's as good as a tennis ball.'

'It doesn't bounce too good.'

'You don't bat too good so you're equal!'

'Try it on the concrete. Bet it'll skid like anything.'

'Hey, where are all the leg-side fielders? Phon! Tommo!'

It didn't take long for the soccer players to see what was going on. Lan saw them coming out of the corner of his eye. He saw the expressions on their faces. He could predict their jokes. Should they pack it in now, he wondered, or tough it out?

Stuff them.

He bowled the grapefruit to Hiroki who, predictably, failed to see it coming. It struck him in the shoulder and thudded into the gum tree.

The soccer players hooted with laughter.

'L.b.w! That's lemon before wicket!' Ryan West chortled.

'Fruit-salad cricket! Must be a Nip version of the game.'

'Willya look at their *bat*!'

'Lemon balls for lemon heads!'

'It's a grapefruit,' Andy Chen retorted, throwing it to Lan.

'Oh, *excuse* us! A grapefruit!'

Adam Morris shoved Lan, grabbing it from his hand. He tossed it to Ryan.

Here we go, Lan thought. Walk away, or pay them back.

Stuff them. He had another one in his pocket.

'Hey, Roki!' He bowled him a gentle one.

'When are they gunna let ya play with real balls?' Adam taunted.

'Nips don't have real balls!' Ryan West jeered.

Hiroki swiped. 'Howzat!' he yelled, overcome with the excitement of contact.

The grapefruit went flying towards Andy at mid-field.

Jason Daniels tried to intercept it and instead barrelled into Andy.

Wham!

'Bonehead!' Andy shoved him back.

'Ya chinko rice boy!'

They leaped on each other.

The grapefruit flew on. It was one of Hiroki's better hits. It hit Mr Thistleton squarely on the left thigh. Mr Thistleton was on playground duty and had strolled across to see what was going on at the eastern end of the oval. He had taught at North Illaba longer than any other teacher on the staff, but it was the first time he had ever been hit by a green grapefruit. Much less one from the bat of a Japanese cricketer, as he told Mrs Thistleton later that day as she rubbed salve on the bruise.

Mrs Thistleton said there was a first time for everything.

Now he gave a yelp of pain. He looked with astonishment at what had hit him. 'What's going on here?'

'Cricket, sir. Sorry, sir.'

'I usually miss,' Hiroki said, still surprised.

'You play with grapefruit?'

'We lost the ball over the fence.'

The siren went for the end of lunchbreak.

Mr Thistleton rubbed his thigh and glanced at the fence. He noted the fruit tree. He looked around for someone to take the blame. He saw the grapefruit in Ryan West's hands. He didn't like Ryan West.

'Come here, West.'

'Please sir, it wasn't me, sir.'

'It never is, is it, West?'

'But I wasn't even battin'! It was him.'

Mr Thistleton clipped him over the ear. 'Blaming your team-mates, robbery, and grievous bodily harm. Not exactly cricket, West. See me after school. The rest of you, get off to class.'

The soccer players departed, muttering their indignation.

Lan was torn. On the one hand, it was terrific to see a dicko like Ryan West being paid out. 'See me after school' meant yard duty. Picking up papers for an hour, probably. Great!

On the other hand, Ryan West hadn't climbed the fence and stolen the grapefruit. He had. How could he let someone else take the rap? As Mr Thistleton had said, that wasn't cricket.

'It was me that nicked the grapefruit, sir,' he confessed.

Mr Thistleton raised an eyebrow. 'Indeed?'

'But our ball's somewhere in that backyard so it's not like a real robbery, more like an exchange. They have our ball and we have their grapefruit.'

'An interesting defence. I'm not sure it would hold up in court. Why didn't you simply go and get another ball?'

'We haven't got another one. And we had to keep practising. We're in training.'

'You ought to be wearing pads,' Mr Thistleton said, rubbing his thigh to emphasise the point.

'We haven't got any pads,' Lan said. 'Or proper bats.'

'We haven't got any proper cricket gear,' Andy said.

'Why aren't you using the school equipment?' Mr Thistleton said. 'Aren't you playing a match during Multicultural Week? Splendid idea, by the way. It's about time cricket was played again at North Illaba. It used to be once, you know. We fielded some excellent teams.'

Lan looked puzzled. 'Mr Drummond said the school didn't have any cricket gear.'

'Oh, I'm sure we do. We've even got a pitch, or the remains of one.' He waved his hand vaguely towards the long grass of mid-oval. 'Mr Drummond's probably forgotten. Our principal, as you've no doubt noticed, is not a cricketing man. I tried to keep the game going after his arrival, but if the support isn't there …' Mr Thistleton cleared his throat. 'Come and see me after school and we'll investigate the dark and unexplored corners of the sports shed. Who knows what treasures we may find.'

He strode off, rubbing his thigh and muttering 'Grapefruit!' to himself.

'Reckon he's right?' Izram said.

'About the gear? Maybe,' Lan said. 'He's the oldest teacher at North Illaba. If anyone knows, it'll be him.'

'Wouldn't it be funny if it's been sitting in the sports shed all the time, while we've been playing with sticks and fruit?'

'Hilarious,' Lan said.

13

'It has come to my attention,' said Mr Drummond, the hairs in his nostrils fairly bristling with indignation, 'that you have chosen an unfortunate name for your cricket team.'

He leaned back in his chair and looked at the two boys standing before him. This time they had not been invited to sit down.

Lan's eyes widened. 'Have we? Why?'

'Why? Why what?'

'Why is it an unlucky name, sir?'

'I didn't say it was unlucky, I said it was unfortunate.'

'Isn't that the same thing?' Lan asked.

'We're not superstitious,' Izram said. 'Well, not very.'

'A lot of cricketers are,' Lan said. 'Spinner — Mr

McGinty — said that when your team's on a lucky streak, nobody changes a single little thing. Not even your socks.'

Izram nodded. 'You don't even do up your shoelaces or comb your hair, otherwise your luck might change. I've never heard of an unlucky name, though.'

'I think it's possible,' Lan said. 'In Vietnam—'

Mr Drummond rapped on his desk. 'Will you be quiet! I said nothing at all about bad luck.' Stupid boys, he thought. Then it occurred to him that they might not speak English at home. The last thing he needed was Ms Trad lecturing him in the staffroom about the special needs of ethnic minorities. He modified his tone. 'I used the term unfortunate in the sense of regrettable. You have chosen a regrettable name for your cricket team.'

Lan kept his expression innocent. This was the part of the meeting he was really looking forward to.

He had enjoyed watching the look of surprise on the principal's face as he and Izram had ticked off all the requirements he'd set them.

They had their players; they'd read out the names. Yes, they had a coach, an ex-Test cricketer, no less: Clarence McGinty. (Mr Drummond, who had never heard of him, failed to look impressed.) They had an official sponsor, the Bukhara Restaurant and Takeaway — Mr Drummond's eyebrows rose — and a tight training schedule in place. They had nets and a reserve to practise in. They'd discovered an old cricket pitch on the school oval that only needed resurfacing. And by a great stroke of good fortune they had all the necessary equipment: bats, gloves, pads, wickets, helmets and balls.

'Ah, yes. Mr Thistleton told me about that.'

He might have told him a little earlier, Mr Drummond had reflected crossly. He wouldn't then have made such a fool of himself two weeks ago banging on about the school's lack of resources while all the time the sports shed was stuffed with sporting equipment nobody knew about.

'North Illaba used to play cricket once, sir,' Lan said.

'So Mr Thistleton informed me.'

'But then it all stopped. About the time you came here, sir.'

'The two events were entirely coincidental. Cricket may not be my cup of tea but I am, of course, only too pleased to see the equipment being used again.'

Mr Drummond returned to the matter under discussion. 'The point is you have your team, you have your coach, and you have your equipment. The thing you do not have is a suitable name. If I am to invite King's to participate in a cricket match to celebrate Multicultural Week I insist that you play under the name of the school.'

'But we are,' Lan said.

'Why would we play under any other name?' Izram asked.

Mr Drummond was momentarily confused. 'I had heard otherwise.'

'What name was that, sir?'

'I had heard that you were calling yourself —' Mr Drummond cleared his throat in some embarrassment — 'er, Nips.'

Lan nodded. 'That's right. Is that a problem, sir?'

'It's written on all the equipment,' Izram said.

Mr Drummond looked aghast. 'The word *Nips* is all over the equipment?'

'Yes, sir.'

'Is that unfortunate, sir?' Lan asked.

Mr Drummond spluttered. 'Well of course it's ... Nips! For heaven's sake, surely you boys know what the word ... What will people ... Whose idea was it anyway?'

'Mr Thistleton's not sure,' Lan said. 'I guess it came from the initials.'

Mr Drummond's head was beginning to spin. 'What's Mr Thistleton got to do with it? Whose initials?'

'The school's, of course,' Lan said patiently. 'Would you like to see, sir?'

The two of them went to the door, opened it and dragged in a large blue-vinyl cricketing bag. 'See?' Lan pulled out a bat and a thigh pad.

On the side of the bag was painted in large white letters *The Nips, North Illaba Primary School*. On the bat and the back of the pad were scrawled the initials *NIPS*.

It had been a wonderful discovery, almost as exciting as finding the equipment itself covered in dust and
cobwebs at the back of the sports shed. Once, long ago
there had been a Nips XI; there was one now; there
might be again. As traditions went, it wasn't much
compared with King's one hundred years of cricketing
glory, but it was a start.

'Mr Thistleton said nippers meant little kids and
nippy meant very fast and powerful, so that's why the
school cricket team was called the Nippers, or Nips for
short. Mr Thistleton said once upon a time all the kids
who went to North Illaba called themselves Nips.'

'So we thought we'd keep the name,' Izram said.

'A proud school tradition,' Lan added.

'Yes, I see.'

'So why is the name unsuitable, sir?' Lan asked.

'Well, I ...' Mr Drummond didn't quite know how
to proceed. He had never even considered the school
initials or the nickname. He had jumped to the wrong
conclusion simply because Lan Nguyen was Asian. The
boy might never have heard the word used as a term of
racial abuse. Should he explain? How could he explain?

'A slight misunderstanding, boys. I wasn't aware
of the historical significance of the name. Nippers.
Nips. And that's what we were called, was it? How
interesting.'

When they had gone, Mr Drummond went to the
window and stared out at the oleanders. He smiled in
satisfaction.

The sight of the principal leering down at him from his office window was enough to frighten the wits out of Ryan West, who was supposed to be emptying bins as part of the punishment set by Mr Thistleton. Instead, he was playing his Game Boy around the side of the toilet block. Caught red-handed, Ryan panicked and his Game Boy fell out of his hand. To his dismay, it disappeared into the sticky depths of the large and revolting bag of rubbish he'd just collected from the canteen bins.

But Mr Drummond wasn't thinking about Ryan West. He was congratulating himself on running a school so completely free of racism that two of his Asian students had never heard the word *Nips* used as a term of abuse.

It was something to be proud of.

It was something to bring to the attention of Ms Trad, who was always complaining to him about what she called racism in the playground.

How wrong she was, thought Mr Drummond, smiling complacently at the oleanders.

14

How could grown-ups take so long to eat a meal? Akram glanced at his watch. They'd been at it for over four hours now, starting with *mezza*: dozens of different appetisers, such as hummos, tahini, kibbe, olives and salads. Then had come kebabs and roast lamb and chicken, rice with raisins, nuts and almonds, all eaten with a scoop of bread torn from the flat loaves of *samoon*, after which they had moved on to figs and sweet custards and baklava.

The women had served the men first, as was the custom, and now they were passing around tea in small glasses and cups of strong, thick, bitter coffee.

Akram loved the eating but couldn't stand the sitting around and the constant yak yak yak in Arabic. His cousins were either too young or too old to play with. The older ones sat with the adults, while the little kids raced around before falling asleep in front of the TV or under the table, despite the music that blared from the stereo.

It was the same every Sunday. What made it worse this Sunday was that for the first time in his life Akram wanted to watch cricket.

Australia was playing Pakistan: it was happening right *now* on television, direct from the Gabba. The crowd would be cheering, the Waughs would be batting, the great Shoaib Akhtar would be smashing the speed bowling record. And what was his set tuned to? The Cartoon Network. Almost four hours of 'Paddington Bear', 'The Flintstones', 'The Jetsons', 'Tom and Jerry' and 'Bugs Bunny'. Every time he'd tried to switch channels there had been howls of protest.

'Aw, not *cricket*! Cricket's boring!'

'Why are you watching *cricket*? It's a stupid game.'

'Turn the cartoons back on!'

They'd be watching at Iz's house, Akram thought. He should have gone there today and watched the match with Iz. Except that his parents would never let him miss the regular Sunday family lunch for such a frivolous reason. Actually, Akram couldn't think of *any* reason why he'd be allowed to miss Sunday lunch, short of death or hospitalisation.

His parents had found it hard to understand his sudden enthusiasm for cricket. They'd teased him about it and no doubt thought he was crazy but they'd raised no objection. They certainly would, though, if he started skipping family get-togethers.

Akram grabbed another Coke from the fridge and a slice of baklava from the tray on the kitchen table. From the drift of voices coming from the dining-room he heard the word *cricket* and knew they were talking about him.

Akram's parents had tried to teach him to read and write Arabic at home but he couldn't be bothered. When his mother spoke to him in Arabic he answered in English. At family gatherings he hung back. He could understand some of what they were saying but he was nervous of joining in.

At times like this he wished his Arabic was a lot better. It was surely in his own interests to know what was being said about him.

He edged towards the door, hoping to lurk around the edges of the group, but Uncle Saeed spotted him. He beckoned him over. Akram went, reluctantly.

His uncle asked him a question. Akram could tell it was a question but since his uncle spoke in rapid Arabic that was all he could tell.

He shrugged, which only elicited more Arabic. 'I don't know,' Akram said. 'I don't understand what you said.'

Uncle Saeed looked at him. Everybody at the table looked at him. 'What are you trying to do, Akram?' his uncle asked. 'Act white?'

Was he referring to his English or to the fact that

he was playing cricket? Probably both. Akram felt angry. It was only a game. All right, an English game, but skin colour had nothing to do with it. He should turn the TV on right now and let his uncle see that the fastest bowler in the world was black.

'If you want to play sport, why don't you play soccer?' uncle number two asked. 'Soccer is a man's game. Arabs love soccer. Everybody in the Middle East plays soccer.'

'*Every*body? Or just the men?' asked his sister Maryam, who never missed the opportunity to make a feminist point.

The men ignored her.

'Or wrestling,' said his cousin Ali. 'Wrestling is very big.'

'Wrestling is disgusting,' said Maryam. 'So macho.'

'Soccer is bigger,' insisted uncle number two.

'There's camel racing,' said uncle number three.

'Are you crazy?' said uncle number two. 'How is Akram going to get a camel? Who races camels around here?'

'I only meant —'

'Better he should kick a ball than hit it with a bat. An *English* bat.'

'It's an Australian bat,' Akram mumbled. 'It's a Kookaburra.'

'Arabs who play cricket might be brown in colour but they are white in spirit,' his uncle insisted.

Akram slid out of the room.

'You should be at Arabic school on Saturdays, not playing cricket,' Uncle Saeed called after him.

'First it is *rats*,' complained Mrs Nguyen. 'Now it is *cricketers*!'

She gave the two words equal emphasis, as if both carried the same degree of horror and revulsion. No, thought Lan: she had managed to make *cricketers* sound even worse.

'I explained about the rats, Ma,' he said.

During one of her cleaning attacks in his bedroom his mother had found the council pamphlet. She hadn't noticed Lan's scribbles on the back, and her English wasn't good enough to translate all the useful information about rodent control. But Mrs Nguyen knew a rat when she saw it. There was a lively picture of one on the front of the brochure, underneath a drawing of the skull and crossbones. She had screamed in horror and rushed from the room, slamming the door behind her.

She and the twins had spent the entire day in the garage. When Lan had come home from school his mother had flourished the brochure in evidence and let him have it.

'So you have rats in your room! You know why? Because of rubbish all over the place, food lying about, old apple cores under the bed, smelly socks! That is where rats breed, in your smelly socks! You think if you put rat poison around your room I not notice? Where is it, hey? Very dangerous to put poison in house with small children! What if they eat it?'

Swipe, swipe, swipe around the ears with the brochure.

He had got out of that one, although it was unfortunate that his explanation was necessarily tied up with cricket. It had established a connection in his mother's mind between rats and cricket.

Which was no doubt why she was now glaring at the poster of Shane Warne on his bedroom wall.

'Your father painted this room just a few months ago. Now look at it!'

Jeez, Lan thought, couldn't a kid have a poster on his own wall?

All right, a few posters.

All right, more than a few.

Okay, two entire walls covered with posters and pictures.

So what? Didn't his mother understand anything about sports psychology? Couldn't she understand how inspirational it was to go to sleep at night and to wake up each morning to those arms raised in victory, to that mouth opened in a shout of triumph, to those legs spread in a Howzat! squat of appeal?

'Why you like this one so much?' his mother asked, jabbing her finger in the direction of the blond hair and the gold earring. 'He looks so angry with his mouth open and yelling. I think perhaps he is not a good person for you to copy, Lan.'

She didn't understand.

'Take down all the pictures before your father comes home.'

'No, I won't!'

'See! Now you answer back to your mother. You never did that before cricket.'

When his father came home, he was sent into the bedroom to view the damage. His eyes roved over the gallery.

'Dad, practically every kid at school has posters of footballers or cricketers or basketball players on their walls. It's no big deal. The marks will wash off.'

Mr Nguyen sat down on the bed and sighed. He was hungry and looking forward to his dinner. He knew why his wife was so upset but he found it difficult to explain it to his son.

'Lan, it is not the walls.'

'What is it then?'

Mr Nguyen glanced at the nearest poster for inspiration and found himself looking into an open mouth and gleaming white teeth.

'Who is this one?'

'Brett Lee. He bowls really *really* fast.'

His father's gaze shifted to the next poster. More blond hair, more white teeth. 'He looks just like this one. No difference. All look the same.'

'Shane Warne's a leggie.'

'A what?'

'A leg-spin bowler. That's what I'm going to be.'

'Lan, you are becoming sports-mad, just like Australians. Sport, sport, sport! It is all anyone in this country cares about, I think. That is why your mother is worried. You come home late from school almost every night—'

'Because of practice! Anyone'd think I was running around with a Vietnamese street gang.'

'You try to change the colour of your hair.'

'Yeah, well it didn't work, did it?'

Thanks to Izram, Lan's black hair was now adorned with a wide front streak the colour of rust. Peroxide might do a good job of bleaching Mrs Hussein's moustache but it had been a total failure at giving him the Warnie look.

'Your mother sees all these cricket books and videos you bring home from the library.'

'She should be pleased I'm even going to the library.'

His father held up his hand. 'Enough. If you were going there for school work we would be pleased. Lan, next year you will be in high school. This is not the time to get into bad habits and neglect your study.'

Cricket a bad habit? Lan was almost speechless with indignation.

Mr Nguyen could smell his dinner. He got up from the bed. 'We want you to work hard and bring honour on the family. These pictures on your wall—'

'I'm not taking them down,' Lan said defiantly.

'If your school marks come down, they come

down. They are a distraction.'

He left the room and went into the kitchen. Lan could hear his mother's voice as she served him dinner. The only English words she used were *cricket* and *Australian*.

They wouldn't think pictures of Vietnamese film stars or tai chi champions were distractions, Lan thought. His walls could be covered with those and they wouldn't say a word.

He marched into the kitchen. 'Find me some posters of Vietnamese cricketers and I'll put those up instead,' he said.

They stared at him in surprise.

15

Practice during the week was at the Denby Street reserve. Every night after school Spinner was there with Larri, waiting for whoever turned up. A few had inevitably dropped out. The demands of home, family and study, or the difficulties of travel meant that others came irregularly. But the dedicated hard-core of players, among them Lan, Izram, Andy, Hiroki, Akram, Tomas, Phon, and Satria were there most afternoons.

Spinner urged them to play fairly, in the true spirit of the game. He taught them to play positively and not be afraid of the ball. He made them throw at the stump from various distances around the field, with Izram usually positioned behind it. Spinner said he had the makings of a fine wicket-keeper. Izram, who shared Lan's dream of hitting boundaries for Australia, was initially disappointed. Who daydreamed of being a champion wicket-keeper?

Spinner took him aside. 'Don't let anyone tell you different,' he said. 'This is the most important position in the team. It needs someone with guts.' Izram was satisfied.

Only two of them — David and Andy — could reach the stump from the boundary with a flat throw, but Spinner said it didn't matter. In schoolboy cricket the ball seldom went to the boundary.

He took them into the nets and taught them to use their feet and drive the ball into the offside net. He'd stand about three metres away and throw gentle half volleys, encouraging them to play the shot. Lan loved net practice most of all. Ian Chappell said that every young player should clock up a thousand balls in the nets each season, and he had a long way to go.

On Thursdays and Fridays, when his mother helped his father in the shop, Lan had to bring the twins with him to practice. At first he'd been embarrassed. He'd even told Spinner he wouldn't come on those days because he had to look after his little brother and sister.

'How old are they?'

'Four and a half.'

'Bring 'em along. Time they learned to toss a ball around.'

It was the highlight of the week for Linh and Tien. Overcoming their initial shyness, they fell instantly in love with Larri and took only a little longer to idolise Spinner. The little dog dashed happily after every ball they threw to him; the old man showed them how to catch, how to form their hands into a natural cup and wrap their fingers over the ball when it came to them. He was teaching the big kids the very same thing, so the twins felt as if they, too, were playing real cricket.

By the second week, Hiroki and Phon were also bringing younger siblings with them to practice. Spinner gave them tennis balls and a plastic stump and even produced a miniature bat. 'Found it hangin' around the shed,' he said. It looked brand new to Lan.

Spinner said it was good for kids to play what he called 'muck-around cricket', to run about and have fun with a bat and ball and not worry too much about winning or losing.

'That's all right for the little kids,' Lan reminded him. 'But we've got a big match coming up.' And he was the captain; he had to do well.

'It's still only a game, mate. You don't want to get too hung up about winnin'.'

Sometimes Lan wondered whether Spinner truly appreciated what he was trying to do.

'It's an *Australian* game, Spinner. That's why all us ethnics are playing it during Multicultural Week. So we have to put on a good show. Our honour's at stake. We can't go out in front of everyone and look like losers. If we do, King's ... everyone will say that Nips can't play cricket and Mr Drummond will say we should have had a multicultural concert.'

'What's wrong with a concert?' Spinner said. 'I like a bit of singin' and dancin'.'

'In a concert everyone's separate. Cricket's a better way to celebrate because everyone plays together and it doesn't matter what nationality you are.'

'You've got a point,' Spinner said. 'But it's still only a game.'

On the nights when the senior players practised, Lan lingered at the nets to watch them. How did some of them make the ball spin and bounce so much, just by flicking their wrist? He studied how they moved their arm and from his position behind the net, he'd try to guess which way the ball would spin.

He asked Spinner to show him the technique.

'Never mind about spinnin' the ball, you just concentrate on getting it to land on the spot.' He saw Lan's face. 'Look, there's lots of different spins.'

'I want to bowl like Shane Warne.'

'Everybody and his dog wants to bowl like Shane Warne,' Spinner grumbled.

'Well, can you show me?'

'Warne's a leg-spinner. You're a natural medium pacer. Stick with it.'

'You said a good bowler should have variety.'

'Accuracy comes first.'

'Why can't I have both? Aw, c'mon, Spinner. Please!'

Spinner sighed. 'Orright, orright. S'pose I'll never hear the end of it if I don't. Come here.'

He showed him the grip. 'The aim's to pitch the ball in line with the stumps. But then the spin turns the ball to the off. Let's look at yer fingers.'

Lan held them out. 'Grace at the library said I had good long fingers. She said I could be a spinner like you.'

Spinner grunted. 'Fingers aren't everything. You gotta have a wrist and shoulders, too.'

'I've got those.'

'You're half-way there then.'

Lan gripped the ball, his third finger bent and his wrist cocked. 'Like this?'

'Take it in easy stages.'

Spinner stood back and watched Lan run up and bowl again and again at the nets. The kid didn't seem to know what easy stages were. On the other hand, although the balls weren't exactly landing on the spot, the kid had a feel for it. He knew what he was trying to do and in time he'd probably get there. Well, blow me brown dog down, Spinner thought. You just never knew.

After his tenth ball, Lan stopped. 'I can't do it. They're too slow and there's no spin.'

'What didya expect? That you'd be a leggie after five minutes?'

'At least I get them in the regular way.'

'True enough. S'pose it all comes down to what sort of bowler you want to be. Nothin' wrong with being a good medium pacer.' Spinner strolled away, as if to see what the others were up to.

Lan gritted his teeth, picked up the balls and resumed his practice.

Spinner watched him out of the corner of his eye. After half an hour he went back and picked up a bat. 'Bowl us a few,' he invited.

'Leggies?' Lan asked.

'Surprise me.'

Lan did. Most of them were donkey drops, most of them missed the wicket, but the two which found their mark did spin a little.

'Not bad,' Spinner said gruffly, putting up his bat. 'You might be a leggie yet.'

Lan's eyes glowed with pleasure. 'Now can you show me how to make the ball go both ways?'

'Gawd, talk about runnin' before you can walk! Top-spinners and wrong-uns, is it? Next you'll be wantin' to do flippers.'

'Cool! What are they? Show me.'

'All in good time.'

'Does Shane Warne bowl flippers?'

'Is the Pope Catholic?'

Lan frowned. 'I'm not sure. I think so. Why do you want to know?'

Spinner grinned. His teeth, Lan noted, looked cleaner than they had that first day in the library.

'It's an expression. It means something's obvious, a dead cert, no question about it. Is the Pope Catholic? Does Warnie bowl flippers?'

Lan liked it. He filed it away for future use.

Spinner was teaching him much more useful English expressions than Ms Trad. He said, 'Then I reckon I should give it a go.'

'Persistent bugger, aren't you?' Spinner took the ball and showed him how it was delivered from under the front of the hand with a flipping of the fingers. 'It looks like a leg-spinner, but it comes flying from below the wrist. See? So it comes faster and lower. With a bit of luck it'll hit the stumps before the batsman can get his bat down to cover it.'

'Wow! Can I try now?'

'It's tough on the hands, mate.'

'Mine are tough. Look.'

You couldn't tell this one, you had to let him learn, Spinner thought. On the other hand, the kid would try anything. It was a good sign. And he could really tweak the ball.

'Send some down. I'll bowl 'em back to you.'

Lan's flippers hit the side of the net, the roof of the net, and occasionally missed the net altogether. After fifteen minutes or so, his face red with exertion and embarrassment, he called a halt. He hoped none of the seniors had seen him. What a loser he must look.

'Had enough?' Spinner called from the other end.

'I'll never be able to bowl this!'

'That's what Shane Warne said when he first tried. Lucky for Australia he didn't give up, eh?'

Lan kicked the grass despondently and didn't reply.

Spinner trudged down the pitch. 'Let's call it a day. Time for me curry anyway. I'm so hungry I could eat a baby's bum through a cane chair.'

Lan couldn't raise his customary grin. He took the net bag and silently began to pick up the balls.

Spinner watched him and then said casually, 'The joker who taught me how to bowl the flipper practised it for ten years before he dared to bowl it in a match. I worked on it for a year before I tried it out. Warnie was twenty-one before he cracked it. Well, I'm off. See you all tomorrow. C'mon, Larri. Tucker time.'

The little dog cocked his head and eagerly trotted after the old man as he headed towards the gate.

Jeez, Lan thought. Ten years! And he was spitting the dummy after thirty minutes.

It was over an hour later when Spinner, Larri at his side, ambled home. Both of them had eaten rather a lot of Mr Hussein's finest beef vindaloo and vegetable bhaji and now the old man was looking forward to a good smoke and a spot of telly before bed.

At the corner of Weller and Denby Streets, he glanced across to the reserve.

'Well, strike me!'

If that wasn't the kid still trying to bowl flippers into the nets. Too far away to tell whether he'd improved, but that wasn't the point. The kid was a stayer.

Spinner burped in satisfaction.

16

David Ho came twice a week to the after-school sessions. He didn't need to come more frequently; he was their best player. In fact, Lan sometimes wondered why he came at all. Most of the Nips were still learning the basic game; David was way beyond that.

He found out why one Thursday when Mr Ho came to collect his son, and insisted on driving Lan and the twins home.

Lan accepted. It was sometimes a long wait for the bus; by the time they got home Linh and Tien were growing tired and cranky and he was so hungry *he* could eat a baby's bum through a cane chair. (The first time he'd used Spinner's expression his mother had looked at him in horror.)

Besides, Mr Ho drove a BMW. The three of them climbed in the back seat.

'It's not like our car, Lan,' Tien said in a loud whisper.

'It's better,' Linh said.

Mr Ho pretended not to hear. 'What do your parents think of you playing cricket, Lan?' he asked conversationally, as he pulled away from the reserve.

Lan shrugged. 'Okay, I guess. They don't really know anything about cricket.'

'They hate cricket,' Linh said.

'Cricket makes them cross,' Tien said.

Mr Ho couldn't pretend he hadn't heard this time. 'Why is that?'

'They think I'm wasting time when I ought to be studying,' Lan said.

'They don't like Warnie. Warnie, Warnie, Warnie!' Linh chanted.

Lan dug her in the ribs to shut her up.

'They think Australians are obsessed with sport,' he explained.

'I'm sure some of them are,' Mr Ho said.

When they got to Dunrobin Street the Datsun was in the driveway. Lan was surprised. His parents didn't often beat him home on Thursdays.

Mr Nguyen came out of the front door just as Lan and the twins were scrambling out of the car. Now it was his turn to be surprised. His children were seldom chauffeured around in a black BMW.

Bursting with excitement, the twins called out to him. He walked down the drive.

Mr Ho switched off the engine and got out the car.

I hope he doesn't expect to be invited inside, Lan thought. He couldn't remember the last time anybody outside the family or anybody non-Vietnamese had got further than the front door. Certainly not anybody driving a black BMW.

He made the introductions while the twins clambered for their father's attention. They hadn't seen him since the previous night and there was a lot to tell.

Mr Nguyen hushed them. He spoke politely to Mr Ho. 'It is very kind of you to drive the children home. Sometimes we worry. Please, would you and your son come inside and meet my wife.'

Lan was astonished.

'Thank you,' said Mr Ho. 'Just for a few minutes.'

Inside, after the flurry of introductions, tea was offered and accepted. Mrs Nguyen brought out the best tea service and they all sat down in the living room. Lan wished he could take David into his room to show him his cricket posters, but knew his parents would regard it as bad manners. Perhaps Mr Ho would too. In the presence of adults, children had to listen politely and speak when they were spoken to.

Mr Ho downed two cups of tea in quick succession, which pleased Mrs Nguyen so much she forgot some of her shyness and actually asked Mr Ho a question in English.

'You like that your son play cricket?'

It was almost the same question Mr Ho had asked Lan.

'I think it's an excellent idea,' he replied firmly. 'Study is important, of course, but it is not the only important thing in life. We shouldn't let work obsess us. I left Hong Kong to have a more relaxed life. I tell David that we have to stop every now and then and smell the roses.'

The Nguyens looked interested but uncertain.

'He is a gardener,' Mr Nguyen translated for his wife. 'In Hong Kong he worked very hard but now he has time to grow roses.'

'And smell them,' Lan added. That was the important point, but he wasn't sure how it was connected to playing cricket.

'I want to smell my roses before I start fertilising them,' Mr Ho said. He chuckled as if he had made a great joke.

'Why is he laughing?' Mrs Nguyen asked.

Her two translators didn't know. 'Just more about gardening,' Mr Nguyen said.

'Why you leave Hong Kong?' Mrs Nguyen asked.

Lan could hardly contain his astonishment. His mother, pouring tea for foreigners in her living room, and asking questions — two of them so far — in English!

'Two reasons,' Mr Ho said. 'There was the changeover in 1997, of course. I didn't want to live under a Communist government.'

The Nguyens nodded.

'And I wanted a less stressful life. In Hong Kong when I woke up in the morning the first thought in my head was how to make more money. I thought about how to make more money all day and came home at the end of the day and thought some more about it, and worked into the night to make more money. I hardly saw my family. We never had time together as a family. Most people in Hong Kong are like this. I came to Australia two years ago because I hoped it would be different.'

'And is it?' asked Mr Nguyen.

'Different, yes. Now I work only half the hours I worked before. But it was hard to start a new life at my age and even harder to realise that now I was the foreigner. But you and your wife know all about that, of course. It is difficult sometimes, isn't it?'

He smiled at Mrs Nguyen and accepted a third cup of tea.

'My family are Chinese, born in a British territory. Now we are Chinese living in Australia. It is a different culture, but we have to accept it and cope. We Chinese have five thousand years of history and five thousand years of civilisation behind us. I want my children to know this and be aware of their ethnic background. But I also know that this is their country now and it is good for them to assimilate.'

He sipped his tea. 'And what is the Australian culture? Most importantly, it is sport. So I encourage my children to play. It is one of the good things about Australia, I think. Life here is not all work and no play and you don't have to be rich to play sport. In Hong Kong it is very, very expensive.'

Lan listened intently to his father's translation. He wanted to be sure his parents understood every word of this.

'Now I am learning golf and I was very pleased when David decided to play cricket. I bought him equipment and encouraged him. He plays for his school but do you know something? He is the only Asian. Very strange. There are many Asian students at the college but none of them play cricket. And then last month David goes to the Illaba Cricket Club and he comes home very happy and says that there is a new team, all Asians who want to learn how to play, and he is going to join them. It is your son's team, of course. Such initiative! And Lan has found an old Test cricketer to coach them. David says he is brilliant. All the boys are coming on well. You must be very proud of Lan.'

Mr and Mrs Nguyen looked dazed. Mr Nguyen, anxious to return the compliment, said, 'And your son, I hear, is the best player in the team.'

Mr Ho shrugged. 'Perhaps it is the tai chi. Tell them, David.'

'I took it up earlier this year and it's really helping me a lot with my cricket,' David said. 'Tai chi's all to do with balance and centre of gravity — well, you probably know about that. It kind of centres your being so you can concentrate better. Dad's golf has improved too.'

'We both go to classes,' Mr Ho said. He stood up. 'Well, it is getting late. We must go. Thank you for your hospitality. My wife and I look forward to seeing more of you.'

The Nguyens waved them goodbye at the front door.

'He must be one of those business migrants,' Mr Nguyen said as the black BMW drove away down Dunrobin Street. 'Only a rich business migrant could work less hours, play golf and drive a car like that.'

'He must have a nice garden, too,' Mrs Nguyen said.

Lan was still recovering from David's surprise revelation. He'd had no idea David did tai chi. He remembered the rude way he'd rejected his own father's offer of lessons, branding it a Nip sport. And now it turned out it was just the thing to improve your cricket. His father would have every right to pay him out.

But his father said nothing. He shut the door and they went back to the living room. Mrs Nguyen started clearing away the tea cups.

'I'm hungry!' complained Linh.

'Want something to eat now,' Tien echoed.

Lan remembered his own hunger. 'How about a takeaway?'

His mother gave him a shocked look, as if he'd recklessly suggested they all go off to the Hyatt for dinner. 'What for? The house is full of food,' she said.

'Which will still be here tomorrow,' Mr Nguyen said unexpectedly. 'Let's try something different tonight.'

'Maybe we could dial a pizza?' Lan said.

'Yay!' The twins jumped up and down in excitement. Would it taste as delicious as it looked on TV?

Mrs Nguyen hesitated. Lan waited for her to say that they never ate pizza before cricket. It was all Shane Warne's fault. He was a bad influence. But then she shrugged and took the twins off to have their bath.

Mr Nguyen closed the door and smiled at Lan. 'Well, what are you waiting for? Go and dial for a pizza.'

17

'It's like chess,' Hiroki said.

Lan frowned. 'How?'

'Tactics are very important in both games. See, in cricket the captain tries to make attacking moves which will help his team win. At the same time, he has to make defensive moves that will stop his team from losing. He has to decide which bowler should deliver which over. He has to decide on field settings. Then he has to keep an eye on the game and move his players around the field, just like a chess player moving the pieces. In both games it's all about trying to gain an advantage over the opposition. When you go in to bat you have to examine the field placings carefully and try to spot the gap in the defence.' He nodded. 'Just like chess.'

Okay, conceded Lan, perhaps it was. But he didn't

play chess and he didn't see how the information would help him face up to King's next month.

They were good. Scary good.

Lan shifted his position on the grass and wondered whether coming to watch them play had been the best idea Spinner had ever had. 'Sussing out the opposition' he called it. 'Scaring the shit out of the Nips,' Lan called it.

He glanced around at their faces now. The college itself had been intimidating enough, with its sweeping tree-lined driveway, vast playing fields and dignified sandstone buildings. Driving up in Mr Ho's black BMW had helped. But then King's had come in to bowl. In less than thirty minutes they'd taken three wickets for nineteen runs.

'Wonder whether you could work it out on a computer?' Hiroki murmured.

'Work out what?'

'Places. Options. Moves. I might give it a try when I get home.'

'Yeah, go for it.' Any little thing that would help, Lan thought.

He glanced over at Mr Ho who was wearing his new golfing cap and sitting behind the wheel of the BMW, reading a newspaper. Maybe King's would think he was the team chauffeur. That ought to intimidate them a little bit. Then he counted all the Range Rovers, Mercs and BMWs parked around the oval and thought it probably wouldn't.

A new King's bowler came thundering in and sent

down a wicked bouncer. Lan could almost feel the batsman's fear as he tried to duck.

Not low enough. Crash! The bowler, scowling ferociously, raised his fist in triumph.

'Death by cricket ball,' muttered Izram.

'Recognise the bowler?' David asked.

'I don't know anyone from King's,' Lan said.

'The cricket club selection try-outs?'

'Oh jeez!'

It was him. The biggest of the blonds. Lan could see the gold chain glinting around his neck. What had they called him? Macca.

'His name's Matthew Macmillan,' David said. 'He's the captain.'

'Oh jeez.'

'They call him Big Mac. Of course. He's pretty deadly, isn't he?'

'He's very fast,' Hiroki observed. 'I wonder *how* fast?'

'The fastest bowler in the world is Shoaib Akhtar. He's Pakistani,' said Izram proudly. 'He bowls at 155 ks an hour.'

Their mouths fell open.

'That's faster than cars on the freeway,' Akram said.

'It's faster than an express train.'

'That's what they call him,' Izram said. 'The Rawalpindi Express.'

There was a thoughtful silence as everyone imagined what it would be like to stand at the wicket, totally defenceless except for a frail little cricket bat, with a missile as fast as an express train hurtling towards you.

Looking around at his team's faces, Lan could see their confidence dribbling away like water from a leaky tap.

'Well, this Pakistani dude doesn't play for King's, does he?' he said. 'And neither does Shane Warne, so we can stop worrying about leg-spinners, too.'

'But *he* does,' said Hiroki nervously, nodding towards the pitch.

'But nowhere near 155 ks,' Lan scoffed. 'Not even half that speed.' He had no idea how fast the King's captain bowled.

'That's still over 75 ks,' Akram said.

'That's still faster than most cars,' Izram said.

Lan dug him in the ribs. This discussion was doing nobody any good at all. He opened his mouth to say something encouraging.

He couldn't think of a single thing. He closed it again.

'Just look at him,' Hiroki moaned.

Lan looked. He didn't know how the batsman felt but he was sitting on the safe side of the stumps and the sight was enough to make him shudder: the tall frame, the blond hair that whipped across his brow, the dark scowl as he stared down his opponent. And that was *before* he started his run-up.

Spinner shuffled up and sat down on a nearby bench, Larri at his feet. The old man had wandered off shortly after they'd arrived — to take Larri for a walk, he'd said. Lan thought he might have gone for a smoke. Sometimes he got desperate. Wherever he'd gone, Lan hoped he'd seen all those wickets falling faster than leaves in autumn.

He was looking smarter these days, Lan noticed. Well, as smart as Spinner was ever likely to be, given his general indifference to fashion and personal grooming. His clothes today actually looked as if he'd run an iron over them. And a hot one at that. The hair beneath the battered old hat he habitually wore was shorter than usual and his trousers were held up by a proper belt rather than an old tie. His shoes had been polished and re-heeled. He certainly wasn't as scrawny — regular meals at the Bukhara had seen to that — and you could look at his teeth without being reminded of old yellow clothes pegs.

Still, he didn't look like the coach of a team who travelled in a chauffeured BMW.

Spinner gestured towards the pitch where to wild shouts of acclaim from the King's supporters another wicket had fallen. 'He reminds me of Thommo.'

'Who's Thommo?' Hiroki asked.

The old man looked disgusted. 'When are you blokes gunna realise that if you want to play the game you have to know the names? Thommo: Jeff Thomson. Two hundred Test wickets and the fastest ever recorded delivery: one hundred miles an hour.'

'What's that in ks?' Lan asked.

'Fast. Bloody fast. And that was when he was bowling with one wing. Record's never been broken. But I've seen Thommo bowl well beyond a hundred when he was at his peak, before his shoulder went. I remember a game in Sydney one day and he bowled this bloke and the middle stump went cart-wheeling all the way back to Marshy.' Spinner cackled. 'How often do you see blokes do that these days?'

'Not often,' said Lan, just as if he'd spent most of his life watching cricket. Who was Marshy?

'There was blood on the wicket when Thommo banged 'em down. He was the fastest and the nastiest.'

'This one is fast and nasty too,' Lan said. 'His name's Macmillan and he's the captain.'

Spinner narrowed his eyes and peered at the bowler. 'Macmillan, eh? Well, he might be nasty but he's not so fast.'

'You said he reminded you of Thommo.'

'Only in looks.'

Lan cheered up.

'And maybe in his run-up. The way he runs flat out every time. And of course, the way he tucks his left arm back across his body. And his follow-through ...'

Lan slumped despondently.

'Who do you think will break Thommo's record, Spinner?' Izram asked.

'Son, records are made to be broken so I don't give a toss. These days a lot of bowlers can bowl the occasional fast one, but that's not the same as chargin' in flat out every time you bowl. That's what Thommo did. He only knew one way to bowl: bloody fast. He had those batsmen starin' death in the face, hour after hour, day after day. Scared the livin' daylights out of them.' He nudged Lan. 'Know what the batsman's trouble is?'

'Yeah. He's not good enough.'

'He's lettin' himself be intimidated.'

For the next forty-five minutes, while King's took all the remaining wickets and the opposition staggered to an early defeat, Spinner analysed the strengths and weaknesses of every player's game, pointed out gaps in the field placements, and crowed 'What did I tellya? Catches win matches!' whenever a batsman was caught.

Lan's spirits lifted. His worst fear had always been total annihilation: that Nips XI would be wiped off the pitch before the first drinks break with some laughable score like all out for 10. Or possibly all out for nothing and a line of ducks on the scoreboard. But this team wasn't posting much of a score either, and yet they were playing for their school against the best in the district. And nobody, as far as he could see, was laughing.

When the innings ended with polite applause, Izram turned to Spinner. 'We know we're not as good as King's, but are we at least as good as the other side?'

It was a question that had occurred to all of them. They looked at Spinner hopefully.

'Ah. Well. Difficult to say.' He scratched his head under his hat. The hat never fell off, Lan noticed.

Perhaps the grease and sweat kept it on. 'We didn't see all their players, we didn't see the whole game, today might be an off day.'

'Yeah, but are we?'

He shrugged. 'On the right day, maybe. Who knows?'

'But on *this* day,' Lan demanded. 'Are we as good?'

Spinner shook his head. He always told them the truth.

Izram said in an anguished voice, 'But they were all out for only sixty-two runs!'

'The best team doesn't always win. They played some interestin' cricket.'

'I'd rather play dull cricket and win the match,' Andy muttered.

'A team's generally got three choices,' Spinner said. 'It can be first. It can be best. Or it can be different. Now in the present circumstances, which d'ya reckon I'm advocatin' for you?' He saw Lan's face. 'I know, I know. You don't want to be different. You all want to bowl like Warnie and bat like Bradman. Maybe you will one day. But right now the thing you got goin' for you is unpredictability. Granted we haven't seen the team bat, but on the strength of the bowlin' today I'd say King's is a pretty predictable side.'

They bowl fast, they take wickets, they win, Lan thought. There was a lot to be said for that sort of predictablity.

Instantly he felt ashamed of himself. Some captain he was. Already Spinner's words had made the Nips look more optimistic. Instead of letting himself be scared off — *intimidated* — by a single innings display of fast bowling, he ought to support the team coach and encourage his players. Like Steve Waugh would do. Okay, he hadn't had very much practice, but thanks to Grace in the library he'd amassed a lot of theory.

'Spinner's got a good point,' he said. 'Do you know what Steve Waugh told the team before they went out to play the West Indies for the first time? When the Windies were the top team and the Aussies didn't know how to beat them?'

'What?' asked Hiroki.

'He said: *Their strength is also their weakness.*'

'Meaning what?' Andy asked.

'Meaning that, you know, like Spinner said, they were the fastest and the nastiest but that was all. Once you got used to that and didn't let yourself get intimidated there wasn't anything else to get you out.' He knew there was a fatal flaw to this argument — what if you weren't in long enough to get used to anything? — but luckily nobody thought to bring it up.

'They were predictable,' Spinner said. 'No variation. Which is somethin' you've got a lot of.' He got to his feet. 'Well, are we goin' over? Congratulate them and introduce ourselves? Only polite, I reckon.'

They walked across to the King's group. The opposing teams kept their distance from each other,

Lan observed: the other school had dumped their gear, set up their chairs and generally made camp some distance away. Did someone tell them to go there or did they just do it?

He was suddenly nervous. Until today the individual members of the King's XI had existed only in his imagination and perhaps that was the best place for them. Putting a face to just one had been unsettling enough.

A sprinkling of parents, players and supporters were packing bags with cricket gear and dismantling card tables and deck chairs. Spinner ambled up to the umpire. 'Well played,' he said. 'You've got some flash bowlers there.'

'Thank you. Yes, we have.' The umpire, a youngish man with flushed cheeks and a smear of sunscreen on his nose, looked up from the score sheets and smiled vaguely. He was wearing a smart Panama hat with a band in King's colours.

Spinner held out his hand. 'Clarrie McGinty.'

'Simon Drinkwater, junior-school sports master.' They shook hands, Mr Drinkwater's eyes going beyond the old man to take in the group of boys surrounding him.

'These are the lads from North Illaba,' Spinner said. 'The ones you're playing in the big match next month.'

'Oh, yes. The headmaster mentioned it to me. A friendly match, isn't it?' He nodded to the boys. 'I guessed you must be the North Illaba team when I saw you arrive.'

That wouldn't have taken much brainpower, Lan thought. How many other teams did they play with a line-up like the Nips? But he could see that Drinkwater was struggling to work out exactly who Spinner was. Too white to be a relative. Too old to be a teacher. Too unfit to be a coach? Probably not for North Illaba.

'You're the sports master, are you, Mr McGinty?'

'Cricket coach.'

Drinkwater smiled. 'And how are the boys coming on?'

'Like the clappers. And after what they've seen here this mornin' I reckon they'll improve even more.'

The sports master gave a little laugh, as if Spinner had said something amusing. 'Good show. Perhaps you'd like to meet our players? I'm afraid some of them might have already gone. They're pretty quick off the mark on Saturdays.' He looked around him. 'Stuart! Tim! Is Matthew there? Ask him to come over, will you?'

Macmillan and two other boys sauntered over. Was everyone in the King's team tall and blond, Lan wondered despondently. It was like an exclusive club with strict membership rules. Up to this moment he'd managed to kid himself that after all the training and practice he was finally getting to be one of *them*, one of those sporting Aussies who knew what to do with a bat and ball. Now he knew he wasn't. He would never, in a million years, be one of these guys.

Then he stiffened. Uh-oh.

'It's them,' murmured Izram.

David had recognised them, too. He gave Lan a nudge.

Drinkwater made the introductions. The three King's players gave no sign of recognition. Perhaps we do all look alike to them, Lan thought.

Spinner was congratulating Macmillan on his play. 'I bet you come from a long line of cricketers,' he said.

'Both my father and grandfather played for the King's First XI.'

'I knew it,' said Spinner.

'Both captains, of course, like Matt,' beamed Drinkwater. 'We have a proud tradition of sporting sons at King's.'

Please, Spinner, don't tell them I'm the captain, Lan prayed.

Spinner clapped him on the shoulder. 'Lan Nguyen, our captain. The match was all his idea.'

The three blonds stared at him impassively.

Well stuff you, Lan thought. He said suddenly to Macmillan: 'We first saw you bowl at the Illaba Cricket Club try-outs. Did you make one of the teams?'

'Yeah.' Macmillan's eyes flicked over him dismissively. 'Did you?'

'I'm playing with this team instead. Nips XI.'

The blond called Stuart snickered.

Mr Drinkwater said quickly, 'Perhaps you'll start

a cricketing tradition at North Illaba. King's has produced a number of Shield players over the decades.
And two great Test cricketers.' He rattled off all the
names.

'Very impressive,' said Spinner abruptly. 'We'll try
and live up to your proud tradition when we play you
next month. See you all then. C'mon, boys.'

He stumped off across the oval.

Taken by surprise, Lan and the others muttered
their goodbyes and set off after him.

'What's up with Spinner?' Izram asked.

'Dunno. Where's Larri?'

Lan spotted the little dog with his nose in a picnic
basket that was lying on the grass in front of a Range
Rover.

'Hang on.' He ran back and scooped him up.
'C'mon, boy. Nothin' in there for you.'

He turned to go and saw Stuart walking towards
them. As he passed he said in an undertone, his eyes
straight ahead, 'We're going to belt the ears off you rice
boys.'

Lan was taken by surprise. Afterwards, he and
Izram thought of a dozen clever things he could have
said in reply.

He caught up with Spinner and the team.

Izram saw his face. 'What's wrong?'

Lan repeated the remark.

'It's called sledging, son,' Spinner said, overhear-
ing. His face was grim. 'He's trying to get up your nose

and demoralise the team. All part of King's proud sporting tradition. The place hasn't changed a bit.'

'You know this school, Spinner?'

'I went to this school, mate.'

They gaped in astonishment. Lan stopped in his tracks.

'But ... why didn't he say your name then? If you went to King's, Spinner, then they've produced *three* Test cricketers, not two. Why did he leave you out?'

'What, a broken-down old bloke like me? Probably never heard of me. You won't find my name on any of the school honour rolls.'

'You must have been in the First XI, though?'

'Nah. I wasn't their sort of cricketer. I wasn't their sort full stop. I went to King's as a scholarship boy. Some of them liked to remind me of the fact.'

Lan recalled the old man's question to Macmillan. 'You knew his grandfather, didn't you?' he said.

Spinner winked at him. 'Get any sharper, mate, and you'll cut yourself. Yeah, I knew him. Come to think of it, his name was Matthew too. Some things never change, do they?'

Mr Ho was standing by the car, trying not to look impatient. As they approached he called out hopefully, 'Everybody ready to go?'

'He wants to get to his golf,' David grinned.

They piled into the car.

'This looks a very fine school,' Mr Ho said. 'Perhaps I'll send you here next year, David. Look at all the wonderful sporting facilities they have. Tennis courts, this fine oval, a swimming pool, I hear. The boys, too, look very motivated. They were by far the better side today, weren't they?'

'It's a school with a proud tradition all right,' Spinner said as they drove away.

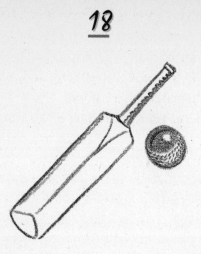

18

For boys who had grown up so sadly deprived, Spinner said, it was an opportunity not to be missed: the First Test, Australia versus India, began on Friday at the Adelaide Oval. They should ask their fathers to take them.

Izram pulled a face. 'My dad wouldn't take me across the road to see India play. He'd call it a waste of good money.'

Spinner shook his head at such ignorance. 'What does it matter who wins? I saw Don Bradman make 201 against India at the Adelaide Oval in '48.'

'I bet Australia won,' Izram said.

'Too right. After a first innings score of 674.'

'My dad wouldn't take me either,' Lan said. Not even if Vietnam was playing, he thought.

'We'll go and see Thursday morning's practice

then. It'll do you good to see how the players train. It won't cost a cent and you get a real close look at them fielding and in the nets.'

'Thursday's a school day,' Lan said, thinking this must have slipped Spinner's mind.

'We'd never get the morning off to watch cricket,' Izram said.

'Misguided in the extreme,' Spinner said. 'They'd cart ya off to a museum or art gallery if there happened to be an international exhibition on.'

He was right, Lan thought. How could he pass up a chance to see the Grand Masters of cricket?

'Not that I'd ever encourage you to skip school, of course,' Spinner said.

'We could leave at recess and I bet nobody'll miss us,' Lan said. 'We'd be back by one.'

'After recess it's Ms Trad,' Izram said. 'She never notices who's there or not. Akka or someone would cover for us if she did.'

'Let's do it,' Lan urged.

'Me ears go crook every now and then so I didn't hear any of that,' Spinner said. 'But just in case anyone's interested, next Thursday mornin' I'll be at the bus-stop outside the mall waitin' to catch the 10.15 into town.'

'Well, look who it is,' Spinner said, as Lan and Izram boarded the bus behind him on Thursday morning. 'Where you blokes off to?'

'Adelaide Oval,' Lan said.

'To watch the training session,' Izram added.

'Well, blow me brown dog down! Me too. Talk about coincidence. You wouldn't read about it, would ya?'

They got off near the Festival Centre and walked across the city bridge. The river sparkled in the morning sunshine, and the air felt fresh with just a hint of summer warmth. The little green and white launch *Popeye* pulled away from the Elder Park landing, full of tourists heading for the zoo further up-river.

Spinner was astonished to learn that neither of them had ever been to the Adelaide Oval. 'One of the prettiest grounds in the world,' he told them, 'with a scoreboard to make your heart swell.'

Lan was glad Spinner was with them. He would never have walked so confidently through the big gates and around the side of the imposing red-brick Bradman Stand.

The perimeter of the oval was alive with activity. Crews unloaded equipment from television outside broadcast vans; caterers staggered between vans, kitchens and large white marquees with stacks of linen and boxes of glassware; food and drinks stands were going up, and men in shirt sleeves strode about muttering into mobile telephones.

Spinner led them around the curve of the members' grandstand and through the brick cloisters to the northern end. A large crowd had gathered at the nets to watch the Indian cricketers. Journalists wearing official badges stood around and chatted knowledgeably to each other. Fans clutching autograph books and cricket bats circled hungrily. Photographers with huge lenses were perched high on vantage points on the northern wall. Most of the attention focused on one particular Indian batsman.

'That's Sachin Tendulkar,' Spinner said, pushing them forward. 'Stand behind him.'

The force and speed of the deliveries and the loud axe-crack of bat on ball stunned Lan. The guy was the smallest of all the players, hardly taller than him, but he carried the heaviest bat and blitzed every ball as if his life depended on it.

A delivery crashed into the netting less than a metre from his nose. Lan flinched and jumped back.

Izram grinned. 'Wicked, hey!'

Lan hardly knew who any of the Indian players were but it didn't matter. Just being this close, being able to see exactly where the feet went, how the bat was gripped, and how the ball was pitched was more than enough.

They watched, absorbed, until Spinner tapped them on the shoulder and said they ought to wander across to the oval and watch the Aussies practise. He handed them each a paper bag.

'Get stuck into that. Can't have you faintin' with all the excitement.'

'A pie!' Lan exclaimed. 'Wow, thanks, Spinner.' What a morning this was turning out to be.

They walked back through the brick cloisters towards the Members' grandstand. Spinner pointed to his left.

'That's the famous Chappell Bar. Somethin' in there you might want to see.'

They followed him into the long timber-panelled room which was empty except for a woman behind the bar drying glasses. Beer cartons were stacked three deep around the walls and Spinner dodged them as he pointed out the highlights of the decor.

'Named for the famous Chappell brothers, of course. You've heard of them, I s'pose? Look on the wall there. That's Ian's cricketing jumper, and there's Greg's bat and his green cap and blazer from the 1978 tour. Now come over and look at this photo. That's the Don. The great Don Bradman.' He rattled off the names of the other players in the old black and white framed photograph.

Lan wasn't very interested. They all looked ancient. They looked like teachers in a school staff photo. None of them looked remotely like Warnie with his earring and bleached flop of hair. He edged his pie a little out of the bag and took a big bite.

Aaargh!

The hot meat scalded his tongue and he juggled it around his mouth, unable to swallow, his eyes watering with the pain. How did people eat these things?

Spinner had stopped in front of another old photograph. The caption read: *Sheffield Shield*

Competition. Players for South Australia. Winners of the Shield 1953. 'Recognise anyone?' he asked.

Lan still couldn't speak. He blinked, trying to clear his eyes, and squinted at the photo, as did Izram, who had already demolished half his pie. It must be all those years of eating curry, Lan thought.

'Gawd, have I changed that much?' Spinner said in mock indignation. 'Look in the back row! Who d'ya reckon that handsome joker is all tizzied up in the state blazer and tie?'

Izram said in surprise, 'It's you, Spinner!'

And there indeed was a younger version of Clarence McGinty, with his head up, dark glossy hair slicked back and shoulders wide and straight, carefree and smiling.

'Wow,' said Izram. 'That's pretty cool, being on the same wall as Bradman.'

'I can't shpeak,' Lan mumbled. Would new skin eventually grow on his tongue? He wiped the tears from his eyes.

Spinner, clearly moved, pulled a handkerchief out of his pocket and handed it to him. 'I s'pose it is somethin' a man can be proud of,' he said modestly. He led them out of the Chappell Bar, his shoulders almost as straight as they were four and a half decades ago.

They emerged from the concrete underpass into sunlight and saw before them the green grass of the oval and the huge scoreboard and the empty stands on the eastern boundary.

'That pitch is a work of art,' Spinner said admiringly. He shook his head, looking about him. 'Strewth, it's a few years since I last stood here.'

On the concourse in front of the grandstand a mob of spectators, some with video cameras, many with bats and autograph books, milled around and crowded the benches close to the white picket fence. Mark Waugh walked right past them and dumped a green and gold cricket bag on the grass.

Lan held his breath. If he'd stuck out his hand he might have touched him.

On the oval, close to the boundary, the other players were kicking a soccer ball around.

'They're not as big as they look on TV,' Izram said.

Lan thought they looked magnificent. And so did the oval, with the flags flying and the spire of the cathedral on the northern horizon and the white seagulls swooping over the brilliant green turf.

The players were having fun with the soccer ball, kicking it wildly, bumping it off their heads and laughing. A ladder was lying on the grass and they ran and hopped between the rungs: good for footwork, Spinner said. The crowd yelled good-natured advice as the players fanned out in a circle and took fielding catches on the run.

'Hey, that's what we do,' Izram said.

Lan pointed. 'Let's move over there and watch Warnie and the others.'

They slid onto a bench just behind Steve Waugh

who was kneeling on the grass in front of the bowler, his bat angled to nick the ball towards the five slips fielders.

A crowd quickly gathered to watch.

When the ball was fielded well there was applause.

When the ball flew over the fence and was caught by a boy in the crowd, there were yells of approval.

When one of the slips fumbled and dropped the catch, someone yelled, 'Don't do that tomorrow!' and everybody laughed.

Lan's heart swelled. He was one of this dedicated army of cricket lovers, the real fans who came to the oval just to watch the team practise, who knew the fine points of the game so well they were able to give the players valuable tips and feedback on their performance.

Fielding practice ended and the team packed up their gear. Kids, many of them decked out in the green and gold World Cup shirts, began to converge on the players' gate, eager to touch their heroes and perhaps get an autograph or snap off a quick photo.

Lan hadn't thought of this. He hadn't dreamed he'd be so close to the action. He should have brought his Warnie poster. What did he have on him that was worthy of being autographed by the world's greatest spin bowler? He'd left his bag and books at school. He had nothing in his pocket but his bus pass.

The only bit of paper he had was the bag holding his meat pie.

Here they came! The twins … Gilchrist … Flemmo … Warnie!

The fans surged forward, thrusting out their bats and autograph books.

'Not now, boys,' Steve Waugh said, sounding just like a captain. 'We'll be more than happy to sign after training.'

He headed towards the players' room. The others followed. The autograph hunters turned their attention to Shane Warne. They had no more luck with him either. He waved all the bats, pen and books aside.

The kids fell back, disappointed but resigned. They'd wait until after training.

Lan couldn't wait. They had to be back at school by then.

Izram said later that it must have been the aroma of the meat pie. He swore he saw Warnie's nostrils flare. Spinner said it might have been the sheer surprise of seeing an Asian face in the Members' Stand. Whatever the reason, the great spin bowler halted in front of Lan.

Lan, too overawed to speak and scarcely knowing what he was doing, held out his meat pie. Or what was left of it.

The famous grin flashed. 'Thanks, mate, but I'd better wait till after trainin'.'

Lan held out the paper bag. Thank goodness there'd been no leakage. Thank goodness it wasn't smeared with tomato sauce.

Warne looked at it and laughed. 'Want me to sign that?'

Lan nodded. 'Please.'

'Well, this'll be a first.' Warne took one of the pens waving in front of his nose, rested the pie bag on his bat and scribbled a few words. He handed them back and strode on.

'Lucky duck!' exclaimed a small boy standing next to Lan.

He and the other autograph hunters sped off in the direction of the nets.

Lan stood, dazed and happy, clutching his pie and the precious pie bag.

'Let's see,' Izram demanded excitedly.

Lan looked at the bag.

The name of the well-known piemaker was printed in blue on one side. The name of the famous cricketer was scrawled across the other: *Shane Warne*. And above it the message: *Keep spinning!*

No four words had ever caused such a sensation at school. Not even the ones that last term had appeared overnight on the walls of the boys' toilet, the first three of which had been *Drummo is a …*

Izram made sure Ryan West got a good look at the bag. 'Know who bought that for Lan, Rye-brain? Bet no Test cricketer ever bought you a meat pie.'

Lan's status shot to skyscraper heights.

He was lucky that Mr Drummond's interest in

cricket was practically zero. Had it been a little higher, he might have found out that two of his students had been at the Adelaide Oval instead of at school.

Someone who did find out was Mr Hussein.

Unlike Mr Drummond (and Mr and Mrs Nguyen), Izram's father read the sports pages of the daily newspaper. He had no difficulty recognising the face of his son in the picture of the crowd gathered behind the Adelaide Oval nets to watch the practice session.

'Izram!' he roared, nearly choking on his breakfast toast. 'What is the meaning of this?'

Izram stared at the photo, aghast. Wasn't there a law against publishing pictures of people without their permission? If there wasn't there ought to be. He'd write to the prime minister about it.

He wondered if he could make it sound like an official school excursion. Would his father ring the school to check?

'Well? What have you got to say for yourself ?' Mr Hussein stabbed his finger accusingly at the picture.

Izram tried to explain how inspirational and educational the excursion had been.

'Indian cricketers!' Mr Hussein exclaimed in disbelief. 'You went to watch *Indian* cricketers in order to be inspired and educated? What stupidity is this?'

He gave Izram a thump.

'Not the Indians, Dad,' Izram said, trying to inject the right note of scorn into his voice. 'We went to see the Australians. Lan got Shane Warne's autograph and we saw Steve Waugh bat. He was in the nets right next to Tendulkar. That's who I was watching.'

Mr Hussein calmed down. 'All right. In that case perhaps you are not stupid.'

Izram seized the opportunity. 'D'you think Australia will beat India in the First Test, Dad?'

'Undoubtedly. Do you think India will succeed when Pakistan has failed?'

'Wouldn't it be great to see the Aussies win, Dad?'

'It would certainly be better than seeing India win. Not that they have the slightest chance, even with Tendulkar.'

'We ought to go and see India get beaten. We could go on Sunday, couldn't we? Spinner could come and Lan and then we'd get the discount price for two adults and two kids which is a really good bargain, Dad. Please?'

When he put his mind to it, Izram could be very persuasive. Which is why on Sunday he and Lan found themselves sitting under a perfect blue sky under the Moreton Bay fig trees, just to the left of the famous scoreboard of the Adelaide Oval, cheering for Australia.

Mr Hussein was so pleased with the match result that he decided to host a special dinner.

19

'This is for you.' Lan handed the invitation to Grace.

She smiled. 'Something else for the noticeboard? You must be looking for a publicity manager by now.'

'It's a Supporters' Dinner. Cricket teams have them before important matches.'

'How exciting!' She looked down at the sheet of paper in her hands.

> *To thank you for your loyal support, the NIPS XI cricket team would like to invite you to dinner at the Bukhara North Indian Restaurant next Tuesday at 7.30 p.m.*
> *RSVP: 8341 9000*
> *Do Not Miss This Prestigious Event!*

'I wouldn't dream of missing it,' Grace said. 'Thank you.'

'It was Mr Hussein's idea. You know, Izzie's father. Even though it's Ramadan now. Do you know about Ramadan?'

Grace did. Grace knew about most things, Lan concluded. It probably had something to do with working at a library.

'Muslims can't eat or drink until the sun goes down. But Mr Hussein says it's also a time when Muslims are supposed to do good and strengthen community ties and he thinks this dinner will do that.'

'I'm sure it will,' Grace said. 'Who'll be there?'

'Our families, and you and Spinner, of course, and a couple of teachers. We don't have that many supporters.'

There had been some discussion as to whether Mr Drummond could be counted as a supporter and whether he should get an invitation. In the end it had been decided that he wasn't, and he didn't. Besides, if he came he'd only insist on making one of his boring speeches.

Ms Trad received an invitation; this was, after all, an Important Multicultural Event at which she should be present. And Mr Thistleton was invited because for the last few weeks he had taken it upon himself to supervise the preparation of the pitch on the school oval. The twenty important metres had been resurfaced and the surroundings regularly mowed and watered by Stan, the school groundsman.

'I meant to ask you,' Lan said. 'Why does Spinner — Mr McGinty — call you WG?'

Grace laughed. 'It's a cricketing joke. There was a famous old cricketer called W.G. Grace.'

'Oh,' Lan said. 'Spinner knows a lot of old cricketers, doesn't he?'

Grace laughed again. 'He was in here yesterday talking about your team. You boys have done him a lot of good.'

'He's not so skinny,' Lan agreed. 'But that's Mr Hussein's food, not us.'

'Oh, I think it's more than the occasional vindaloo,' Grace said.

Lan left the library, shaking his head. The occasional vindaloo! He'd make sure Grace sat near Spinner at the Supporters' Dinner so she could see just how much one old man could put away.

Her remark about publicity had given him another idea too.

For someone who hadn't eaten or touched a drop of water all day and couldn't for at least another fifteen minutes, Mr Hussein was in a jovial mood. He'd already made two speeches of welcome and Lan had a feeling he was about to make another.

Any more speeches, he thought, and they might just as well have invited Mr Drummond.

But everybody seemed to be enjoying themselves, even the families of Akram and Jemal who, like the Husseins, would be fasting until the sun went down. Everybody else had eaten poppadums and samoosas

and bhajis, and drunk beer and jugs
called *nimbu-pani*.

'I thought you said you didn't have
porters,' Grace said, smiling at him from acro
table.

Lan grinned back. They might only fill a few rows
in the Bradman Stand but in the Bukhara tonight it was
almost a full house. And a noisy full house at that. A
few people had been shy and reserved at first, but that
hadn't lasted long. The tables were full of friends and
families chatting and laughing and it was all because of
cricket.

Last term he had only counted Izram and Andy as
real friends. Now he felt close to all the Nips, even the
ones who hadn't made the team. Their parents had
become acquainted, too. They'd acted as chauffeurs
and bumped into each other at the Denby Street nets.

But it was backyard cricket which had done the
most to bring parents and players together. Hiroki had
smashed Mrs Chen's bathroom window — twice —
and the delicate shrubs that lined the Faudzi's driveway
would probably never flower again. Akka had dived
into the Catano's shade house while trying to catch a
hat-trick ball, and Iz had put a leg through the fibro
roof of the Yoshidas' carport while retrieving a sixer.
The resulting damage and visits to the doctor had
brought all families together in a heart-warming way.

Lan wished his own parents had been a little
more involved but they always seemed to be working.

his cricket posters. And
... was really something.
...dian curries!

... feet again, rapping on a

... Lan murmured under his

...ng next to him, said, 'That's
what ... are all about, mate. Nothing
but non-stop speeches. The punters expect it. They'll be
callin' on you next.' He took up his glass and leaned
back in his chair in expectation.

It had never occurred to Lan that he might have to
make a speech. He sat, frozen with apprehension, Mr
Hussein's words washing over him and only dimly
comprehended.

What was he saying? Announcing the team. '... the
selection was made by the chairman of selectors,
Mr Clarrie McGinty; the team coach, Mr Clarrie
McGinty; the team captain, Mr Lan Nguyen, and the
team manager, Mr Lan Nguyen ...'

'That's you!' Linh called delightedly, waving a
chappati at Lan, amid the laughter and applause.

Mr Hussein read out the names: Andy Chen,
Akram Rajavi, David Ho, Lan Nguyen (captain),
Hiroki Yoshida, Tomas Nunez, Izram Hussein (wicket-
keeper), Satria Basalama, Phon Phimonyanyong (here
he stumbled; 'Now I sound like an Australian cricket
commentator,' he joked), Jemal Faudzi, Sal Catano;

twelfth man, Rikki Koh. 'Have you ever heard a list of names like that?' he demanded. 'This team will make cricketing history on Thursday!' He gave the table in front of him an enthusiastic thump.

When the applause died down, Spinner got to his feet. 'It behoves me to say a few words on this auspicious occasion,' he said solemnly. Lan hoped he'd say a lot of words and leave nothing for him to add.

Spinner cleared his throat. 'It's been a long time since I've played cricket and a long time since I've wanted to. And over the years a lot of people have asked me why I gave it up. Let me just say it wasn't the game itself, it was the way it was sometimes played and the people who sometimes played it. And that's all I'm sayin' on that subject. But once cricket gets in yer blood it tends to stay there, as some people here tonight will know.'

Grace and Mr Hussein beamed and nodded their agreement. It was true, Lan thought, and how lucky for the Nips that it was. Without Grace he wouldn't have known what books to read and he wouldn't have met Spinner at all. Without Mr Hussein the Nips wouldn't have Spinner as a coach. Although since the King's match he'd been wondering about that. Perhaps Spinner's feelings about his old school had been as much an incentive as Mr Hussein's vindaloos.

'Some people get a bit possessive about the game. Well, they're mugs because cricket doesn't belong to them. Or anyone, for that matter. Some people think they're bigger than the game and some people think winning's the only thing and they're mugs too, because it's the playin' that's important, not the prize at the end.

'That's not to say these lads won't be goin' out on the pitch on Thursday and doin' their best to win, but it doesn't matter to me if they don't, as long as they play the game and walk off with pride. They've come a long way in a short time. That's an achievement in itself. But best of all, they're playin' for the right reason, because true sportsmen play for the love of the game. They wouldn't've put up with a bad-tempered old codger like me if they didn't. I hope they go on playin' for years to come. I hope some of 'em play for Australia. And why not? This is the land of the fair go and the land that loves the battler.'

'Hear! Hear!' cried Mr Thistleton.

Spinner raised his beer glass. 'To the Nips.'

'To the Nips!' The toast rang out around the restaurant.

Mrs Nguyen whispered to Lan, 'Why they love only the batter? Why they not love bowlers too?'

Lan tried to explain. He wasn't quite sure what a battler was. 'He means Australians often cheer for someone who's not winning.'

'Do they?' This had hardly been Mrs Nguyen's experience but then, she had not watched very much cricket.

It must be his turn to speak now, Lan thought nervously. He couldn't think of a single thing to say.

He'd stammer and stutter. He'd forget all the people to thank. He'd get all his words mixed up. He'd look a complete idiot. 'Is this the captain?' people would ask themselves in dismay.

To his surprise, Mr Ho, who was at one of the tables along the end wall, said he wanted to make an announcement. Lan hoped it was a long one.

Mr Ho stood up, looking very smart and relaxed in a dark green shirt and well-pressed slacks. He cleared his throat and adjusted his glasses.

'My son David doesn't attend North Illaba school but he is a Nip.' He glanced around at all the faces, some of which seemed a little uncomfortable. 'Some of us would perhaps prefer that our sons did not play under this name, but I think they are right. First, it is a joke and it is important to keep one's sense of humour. Second, it is the name of the school's original cricket team and tradition is very important in cricket.'

'Hear! Hear!' cried Mr Thistleton.

'Sport can teach valuable life lessons. That is why I'm a Nips supporter and why I and Mrs Nguyen have a special presentation to make to the team.'

Lan nearly fell off his chair. His mother!

Mrs Nguyen stood up and gave a shy nod.

Mrs Hussein and Sheela carried in a large cardboard box.

'Official team uniforms,' Mr Ho announced.

There was an excited buzz as white carrier bags were distributed. Inside the one with his name on it was

184

a pair of long cream pants and a short-sleeved polo shirt. On the pocket, beautifully embroidered in green and gold, were the intertwined initials NIPS. He grinned. And there on the right sleeve, just like a real professional's, was the name of their sponsor: Bukhara.

Lan, speechless, looked across at Izram. He looked gobsmacked too.

'I provided only the material,' Mr Ho said, waving his hand dismissively. 'This was nothing. It was Mrs Nguyen who did all the sewing.'

There were loud murmurs of appreciation and applause.

'Splendid, splendid!' cried Mr Thistleton.

'Such beautiful work,' Grace said admiringly, inspecting Lan's shirt.

'I found out everybody's size and kept it all a secret,' Ms Trad told her table excitedly.

'With all this cricket Izram has got so skinny,' Mrs Hussein exclaimed. 'Two whole sizes he has gone down!'

Across the room, Akram was delightedly examining his new uniform, a wide grin splitting his face. At last he was going to be dressed in exactly the right clothes!

Mr Nguyen beamed at his wife in pride. She sat down, blushing.

Still Lan couldn't speak. He had a picture in his mind: his mother, inside the garage, sewing; himself, outside, banging the ball against the wall, complaining.

He looked at his mother. 'Thanks, Ma. These are cool.'

She patted his hand. 'You play well in these clothes, yes?'

He nodded. Surely now he must get up and say something.

'I speak now, please.' A small woman with a delicate, pretty face and dark soulful eyes was standing up.

Lan sighed with relief. Everybody but him seemed to want to make a speech.

'My name is Isabel Nunez. I am the mother of Tomas. Excuse me please, my English is not perfect.'

Everybody smiled at her encouragingly. Very few in the Bukhara spoke perfect English.

'I and my husband would like to say thank you. Before cricket my son did not want to go to school. He had no friends. His English was poor. Now all that has changed. We are pleased that he is a Nip. Thank you.' She sat down.

Everybody clapped. 'Good show!' said Mr Thistleton.

'We're wogs but Salvatore is a Nip too,' called out Mr Catano. He was a short burly man with a curly helmet of hair and a permanently cheerful face. 'He's the first person in the family ever to play cricket. I said to him, "Why are you playing that stupid game? Italians play soccer." He said, "Dad, I've got something to tell you. I've always hated soccer."' He shrugged and his face took on an exaggerated expression of sorrow.

There was laughter. Mr Rajavi stood up and said, 'Some Arabs think it is a stupid game too. But I am not one of them. This is Australia and I am happy for my son to play an Australian game — even if he is a dangerous fielder to have in your backyard.'

The Catanos all laughed good-naturedly. Mr Catano held up his glass and said 'Saluti!'

Mr Rajavi looked hopefully at his watch.

Mr Hussein consulted his watch too, and thumped the table. 'My goodness, yes! Now we eat and drink!'

Spinner's nostrils twitched appreciatively as large platters of meat, poultry and vegetables, and side dishes of chappatis, dahls, pickles, chutneys, yoghurt and rice were carried in. 'I'd be as hungry as a black dog if I had to wait all day for this,' he said.

Lan grinned. Suddenly he wanted to speak. He had important things to say and as captain it was his responsibility to say them. He jumped up and looked appealing at Mr Hussein. Izram's father smote his forehead.

'I've forgotten the captain! Forgive me, Lan.' He rapped on the table for attention. 'One more minute! A few words from the young man who started all this.'

All eyes were on him now. Lan took a deep breath. 'This is the last speech.' He looked at Mr Hussein. 'At least I hope so.' Everybody laughed, including Mr Hussein, who threw up his hands in surrender.

'Thank you all very much,' Lan began, and then the words came easily. He thanked everyone he could think of: his mother, Mr Ho, the Husseins, all the other parents, brothers and sisters, Grace, Spinner, Ms Trad, Mr Thistleton, and his fellow Nips. He thanked Larri for being the team mascot and the parents who would provide the lunch on Thursday and Shane Warne for inspiring him to be a spin bowler. Then he stopped because he was beginning to sound like one of those annoying actors at the Academy Awards.

He had intended to say something macho about going out there on Thursday and winning. But he had come to realise that this audience didn't much care whether the team won or not. In their eyes, their sons were already winners.

The door of the restaurant opened and two men came in. One of them carried a large camera bag.

Relieved, Lan said, 'I think someone wants to take a photo for the paper.'

'Good show!' said Mr Thistleton approvingly.

20

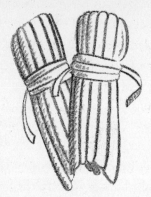

Lan lay in bed watching the daylight brighten around the edges of the blind. It was going to be a perfect day for cricket. Last night's forecast had been for clear skies, light breezes and a maximum of twenty-five degrees.

He'd stayed awake for what seemed hours last night, endlessly plotting today's game in his head and trying to figure out a winning formula. The only one he'd come up with was take a lot of wickets, make a lot of runs, don't do anything stupid. He wondered if Steve Waugh got a good night's sleep before an important match.

Yesterday Hiroki had brought his laptop to training. He and Lan had entered all the relevant data into the program Hiroki had devised and the computer had worked out the optimum batting order. They'd called

Spinner over to look at the information, certain the old man would be dazzled by technology unheard of in his day. Spinner had put on his glasses and looked at the screen without comment. Then he'd pulled from his pocket a crumpled piece of white butcher's paper that smelled strongly of salami. On it he'd scribbled his own batting order. It was the same.

Lan was glad computer and coach were in agreement. It was one less thing for the captain to worry about.

Shortly after he'd been elected captain and feeling the weight of responsibility heavy on his shoulders, Lan had gone to the library, found the home page of the Australian Cricket Board and fired off an email question: *What are the important duties of a captain in school cricket?* Back had come an answer:

Remain cheerful.

Go for a win and when that's not possible fight for a draw.

Never give up hope until the final ball has been delivered.

It didn't sound like much, but Spinner said if Lan did all that he'd be doing well. 'But there has to be more to it than that,' Lan had argued. 'Haven't you got any good advice, Spinner?'

The old bowler had scratched his jaw. 'How about this? Never overestimate the strength of your opponent.'

It had puzzled Lan at first; surely the old man

meant *underestimate*? But now he knew what Spinner meant. It was easy to get freaked out in cricket. It was especially easy when you were up against a school that had been playing cricket for well over a hundred years. The King's First XI all carried the distinctive air of superiority, but did that mean they *were* superior?

Yes, it did. They were bigger, blonder, richer and they won every match they played.

Lan groaned loudly and pulled the pillow over his head.

The twins carefully opened the door and peered in at him. 'Are you sick?' Linh asked.

'Aaarghmomngbh!'

'What?'

He threw the pillow at them. 'Go away.'

'You're in the paper,' Tien announced.

He flung the covers aside and leapt out of bed. How could he have forgotten?

'Spinner's in the paper too.'

Lan raced into the kitchen, the twins skipping after him.

'Why aren't we in the paper? We was at the party too.'

'You're not famous and you don't play cricket.'

'Yes, we *do*!'

The newspaper was lying on the kitchen bench, folded back to the relevant page. His father must have gone down to the deli on Willmott Street and bought it before he left for work. Lan snatched it up.

'*Mystery Spinner bounces back after half a century,*' said the headline. Underneath, spreading across four columns, was a picture which had been taken at the Bukhara on Tuesday night. The caption read: *Mr Clarrie 'Spinner' McGinty surrounded by members of NIPS XI, the North Illaba Primary School team he is coaching.*

Lan peered at himself. Hmm, not bad!

'Very nice picture,' his mother said proudly. 'I buy lots of papers today and send it to everyone we know.'

Lan sat down and tried to clear a space. The kitchen bench was covered with bowls of chopped prawns and shredded chicken, onions, garlic, eggs, bottles of oil, bean sprouts and assorted vegetables; on the stove a wok bubbled and hissed.

'What's all this?'

'I make spring rolls for your International Food Day.'

Lan groaned. His eyes skimmed down the story: *One of the cricketing sensations of the 1950s …Test player who came from nowhere with an extraordinary talent … rapidly became one of the world's most destructive bowlers … sudden surprise retirement … out of obscurity and self-imposed exile, McGinty has emerged to coach a team of ethnic schoolboys, many of whom have never played cricket before …*

'Have some noodle soup,' his mother urged.

'No, thanks.' The last thing Lan wanted this

morning was noodle soup. He wanted a Shane Warne breakfast: a Vegemite sandwich. 'Have we got any Vegemite?' he asked hopefully.

'No.'

'I keep asking you to buy some.'

'Have some noodle soup. Very good for cricketers.' She put a steaming bowl in front of him.

She was trying so hard, Lan thought.

'Thanks, Ma.' He picked up his spoon. His eye skipped to the end of the story. A bit about all their ethnic backgrounds ... a quote about how he'd thought up the idea to celebrate Multicultural Week because 'I didn't want to do any more dancing in national costume' (Mr Drummond would be cross) ... their efforts to put a team together ... its rejection by Illaba Cricket Club ... details of today's match at the school (Mr Drummond would be pleased) ... and then the bit he'd hoped would be there:

> *Little did the boys know when they asked McGinty to be their coach that the ex-Test cricketer is an old scholar of King's College. But he says he has no divided loyalties.*
>
> *'Australian cricket, at all levels, is almost exclusively white and a bit too elitist,' McGinty said. 'People who want the game to survive in this country ought to be encouraging kids like this to play.'*
>
> *And how does he think the rookie NIPS XI will*

perform today against the team who last year won the Intercollegiate Cup?

'They'll surprise a lot of people,' he predicted.

Lan, satisfied, put down the paper. The point of the story hadn't been self-publicity or even to focus attention on the match. The newspaper wouldn't have sent a journalist and photographer out to the Bukhara on Tuesday night for that. They'd come because of Spinner; he was the hook. Lan had known that when he'd phoned the paper.

He hoped Mr Drinkwater and the whole First XI at King's read the story. He hoped the headmaster had hung his head with shame and rushed out with a pot of gold paint and added the name of Clarence McGinty to the honour roll.

'Good soup, Ma.' He finished, and pushed the bowl aside. She smiled and nodded.

'I want Vegemite,' Tien was whining as he left the kitchen.

As he got ready for school he went over in his mind what he'd say in the dressing room before the Nips took to the field. The school didn't actually have a dressing room. Heck, until this week they didn't even have a field, but that wasn't important. It was the words that counted. They had to be encouraging and, most of all, motivating.

'If you think you can or if you think you can't, you're usually right,' Spinner had said. 'It's all in the state of mind. So make sure you all take to the field thinkin' that you can.'

Lan packed his cricket whites carefully in his bag. Before he'd gone to bed last night he'd put them on and crept into the bathroom to see himself. He had to stand on the toilet seat to see his bottom half and when he did he couldn't see his head and shoulders, but his legs and torso looked so splendid it was hard to tear his eyes away.

He took his autographed pie bag down from the wall where it was pinned to his Warnie poster and put it carefully between the folds of the clothes.

Before he left the house he lit a stick of incense and put it with the others in front of the family altar. He said a little prayer and touched the photograph. 'Wish me luck, Grandma.'

'We all wish you luck.'

He turned. His mother was at the door to the kitchen. She said, 'I see you later at school. Mrs Ho is driving me and Mrs Nunez.'

'Yeah?'

'Oh, yes. We have so much food and cooking things. Too much for the bus.'

The twins followed him to the front gate.

'Will Larri be with Spinner at the cricket?' Linh asked.

'Is the Pope Catholic?' Lan said.

21

Mr Drummond had been caught on the hop. He had, of course, intended to show the proper amount of interest in the sporting activities on the school oval today. He had in mind greeting the visitors from King's, delivering an appropriate speech, watching the first five minutes of the game and then disappearing to the comfort of his air-conditioned office until lunch. He was looking forward to that. The international food was, in his opinion, the whole focus of the day, anyway. Nobody except perhaps old Thistleton was much interested in a bunch of schoolboys whacking a ball around an oval.

The first shock of surprise had come on his arrival this morning. He'd hardly set foot inside the administration block before Mrs Moody in the front office all but flung herself on him, waving a stack of yellow phone message sheets. Her face was alight with excitement.

'Everybody's been ringing! Newspapers from all over the country, the television, the radio stations! Even *A Current Affair*!'

'Good heavens! What for?' He rapidly ran over in his mind the list of possible disasters: fire, massacre, kidnapping, food poisoning ...

He suddenly went pale. The oleanders! Some brainless child had eaten a piece of them and perished. Mike Moore would make mincemeat out of him. *'Isn't it a fact, Mr Drummond, that the victim's parents begged you to cut the bushes down months ago?'*

'Who was it?' he asked hoarsely. Not one of the students who spoke a Language-Other-Than-English, he prayed silently.

'And isn't it a fact that the victim had a poor command of English and might not have understood verbal warnings?'

Mrs Moody shrugged. 'I didn't get the name. There's a number for you to call back.'

Even Mr Drummond thought this was treating the matter a bit casually. 'Well, I do think you might have found out who it was before I call, Mrs Moody.' Stupid woman! He headed for his office, his agitation growing. 'Are the police coming?'

'I don't think so.' A puzzled Mrs Moody followed him down the corridor. 'Why would the police be interested?'

The principal stopped. He felt a faint flickering of hope. 'Just what are we talking about, Mrs Moody?'

'Cricket, Mr Drummond.'

'*Cricket?*'

'The match today. Didn't you see the paper this morning? I'll get it for you.'

Mr Drummond sank into his office chair just as the telephone rang. It was someone called Burridge from the Illaba Cricket Club offering the services of an umpire for today's match. No sooner had he hung up than it rang again. This time it was the sports desk at the ABC asking if he could put them onto someone called Clarrie McGinty.

The phone rang non-stop for the next ten minutes, during which time the principal managed to read the story in the morning paper.

Mr Drummond didn't give a fig for some old cricketer but if the national media was about to descend on North Illaba he was determined the school would rise to the occasion. He had little more than an hour. He sprang into action.

Classes were cancelled, teachers summoned, work gangs organised. Flags and banners were strung up around the oval. The old sports day marquee was hurriedly erected at one end of the oval to serve as the refreshment tent. Teachers were ordered to move their cars out onto the street to make space for a media car park. The school recorder band was assembled and told to practise 'Advance Australia Fair' in the girls' shelter shed until they got it right.

Ryan West, Adam Morris and their friends were

detailed to lug benches and chairs from all over the school to provide seating. 'For parents and the media,' Mr Drummond stipulated. 'Students can sit on the grass.'

'Catch me watchin' stupid cricket,' muttered Ryan, but not too loudly. The others paid him no attention anyway. His status was sinking faster than the *Titanic*. Incredibly, the wild rumours which had circulated at the beginning of term seemed to be coming true.

As it turned out, Ryan had no choice. Mr Drummond announced that he expected everybody on the oval to support the school team.

At a quarter to ten the King's College mini-bus drove into the car park. Mr Drummond noted their arrival from the front office and hastened down the steps to welcome them, just in time to hear a young red-headed television reporter speaking earnestly to camera: '... two schools at opposite ends of the economic spectrum. Here at North Illaba Primary, English is taught as a second language in overcrowded classrooms and its only sporting facility is a scruffy unpretentious oval. Its bare bitumen playground is in stark contrast to the leafy campus and ivy-covered walls of prestigious King's College ...'

Mr Drummond tapped her on the shoulder. 'Young lady, we have dozens of trees and an abundance of grass on the other side of the administration block. Might I suggest you go and film there?'

'Cut!' the reporter said. Moving away, she murmured to the cameraman, 'We'll do it later. Get the rich kids coming off the bus.'

The King's players behaved as coolly as if they were always greeted on arrival by television cameras. They hadn't expected to be impressed by anything at North Illaba and they certainly weren't going to start in the car park.

'A bit of media excitement here this morning,' Mr Drummond said jovially, shaking Mr Drinkwater's hand. 'You probably saw the story in the paper.'

'Yes,' said Mr Drinkwater. It had been the chief topic of conversation in the headmaster's office before he'd left this morning. 'You see what this McGinty's saying about King's, don't you?' the headmaster had demanded, stabbing the paper. 'We're white and we're elitist.' Mr Drinkwater hadn't been quite sure what the headmaster had expected him to do: suddenly find some Asian scholarship students and throw them into the First XI?

'He's referring to Australian cricket, Headmaster. See, he says —'

'He means King's! He's got a chip on his shoulder about something. Why isn't he on the school honour roll, anyway?'

Mr Drinkwater didn't know.

'Well, just make sure we win.'

'Oh, there's no doubt about that, Headmaster.'

The only thing in doubt was the margin of the

win. Mr Drinkwater hoped it wouldn't be too embarrassingly large. There was no fun in shooting fish in a barrel.

Out on the oval, Spinner was inspecting the pitch with Larri and a bunch of eager reporters at his heels. Gawd, why couldn't they leave a man alone? All these flamin' questions! Didn't they have anyone more interestin' to interview than an old has-been cricketer? What had he been doin' for the last five decades? Mindin' his own bloody business, for one thing. Strewth, he had trouble rememberin' where he last put his glasses down, let alone what'd happened fifty years ago on a Test wicket. Yes, of course he still followed the game. He hadn't given *the game* away, he just had a few problems with the way it was played sometimes. A photo? Bowling a spinner? Nah, he was past all that. Well, orright, he just happened to have his old baggy green cap on him. Found it last night stuck away in a trunk with a lot of other stuff. Could they make sure Larri was in the picture?

In the boys' toilet block which was serving as a changing-room it was the moment for Lan's big speech. He looked around at the team, together in their whites for the first time. A few, like Andy and David, looked calm but they were in the minority. Most of the team looked nervous. Even Izram, whose confidence and enthusiasm seldom waned, was biting his fingernails. Through his new wicky gloves.

Lan decided to make it brief and snappy and positive.

'Okay, Nips, listen to me,' he said briskly. 'I've got three important things to say to you and that's all. Three things that'll make us winners.'

Hiroki stopped staring glassy-eyed at his bat, and lifted his head. They all gazed at him in expectation.

'You bowlers,' Lan directed his gaze at them, 'remember to bowl to your field, okay? Second, fielders. Stay alert, don't drop any catches, and give it all you've got. Catches win matches. Do that and we can knock King's over like a row of empty drink cans. That's all. Okay, let's go.'

He headed for the door.

'You said three things.' Izram called. 'What's the third important thing that'll make us winners?'

Lan stopped. 'The third thing? The third thing is …' He frowned, trying to remember. He'd read it only last night. 'I've forgotten,' he admitted. 'Let's go anyway.'

22

The two captains went out to meet the umpires, Clarrie McGinty and Simon Drinkwater.

Matthew Macmillan had the toss. He flipped the coin. 'Call!'

'Heads,' Lan said.

The coin fell and lodged in the soft grass at an angle of about sixty degrees. Lan couldn't see which face was uppermost. Before anyone had a chance to react, Macmillan had leapt forward and grabbed the coin. 'Better do that again,' he said cheerfully. 'Want to call again?' He flipped.

The coin was already in the air. 'Heads,' Lan called.

This time the coin landed cleanly. Tails.

'We'll bat,' Macmillan said.

'Right,' said Drinkwater. 'Thirty overs, no bouncers, batters retire at fifty runs.'

As they walked off, Spinner murmured to Lan, 'Watch out for Blondie. That first call was heads.'

Lan shrugged. 'It's not that important.'

'It's not cricket,' Spinner grumbled.

The umpires took up their positions, Larri sitting as usual at Spinner's feet. Nobody from King's dared to suggest he shouldn't be on the field. Who was going to argue with an ex-Test cricketer?

The spectators arranged themselves around the boundary, sitting cross-legged or lying on the grass. A sprinkling of parents had brought folding chairs; others sat on the school benches.

The two King's batters walked on to the pitch, Macmillan at the striker's end. Mr Thistleton and Mr Burridge (who had come to umpire and found himself pressed into service as a scorer) took up their score sheets and pencils. The two twelfth men armed themselves with chalk and stood either side of the scoreboard. And to enthusiastic applause, fast bowler Andy Chen came running in to deliver the first ball.

Eight runs off the first over: it was not an encouraging start.

Perhaps it was because over the last few months he'd read so many cricket books and poured over so many match reports that Lan found himself writing the game in his head as it unfolded. It had been hard to remember all the names as he'd successively shaken hands with the members of the King's team, but a glance at the scoreboard kept him on track.

King's openers Mark Perry and Tim Morton made immediate use of the batting strip, blazing away to a rip-roaring start and frustrating the Nips bowling attack ...

Frustrated was right. Between them, Andy and David, the opening bowlers, had sent down six overs without claiming a wicket. Hiroki and Tomas had an equally disappointing result. If that wasn't bad enough, King's were piling up the runs at a rate of seven per over.

At least the media had disappeared. Having interviewed Spinner and got their background footage, most were gone by the first ball, much to Mr Drummond's dismay. Not even the promise of a curry lunch had been enough to keep them.

Seventy off ten overs. Things looked grim.

Their strong partnership sent King's confidence soaring into the stratosphere ...

If it wasn't already there, Lan thought. Perry made his fifty runs and swaggered off the pitch, waving his bat to acknowledge the applause. Easy-peasy! That's what the score would be saying to the spectators and especially to the other King's players lounging around on the edge of the oval. Just in case they hadn't worked it out for themselves.

Lan tried to keep his confidence high as Morton batted his way towards his half-century. Then their luck changed. Hiroki and Tomas took two quick wickets in their fourth overs, Morton run-out from an amazingly accurate throw by Phon, the other an l.b.w.

'It often happens,' Spinner said. 'After a big partnership you often get 'em out one after the other, just like that. Down like flies. They get complacent, y'see.'

Fourteen overs gone and eighty-four runs on the board. Lan decided it was time to bring himself on.

If Lan had his sights set on anybody it was Stuart Wilson, the second and nastiest of the three blonds.

'Go for broke,' Izram muttered, crouching behind the wicket. He hadn't forgotten Wilson either.

Quietly relaxed, supremely confident and perfectly balanced, Second Blond stood at the wicket, prepared to move either forward or back according to the length of whatever unpredictable delivery should come his way. He barely glanced at the field placings.

Lan walked back for his run-up. He put his hand in his pocket and stroked the pie bag for good luck. Somehow he knew the spirit of Warnie would come through.

He launched into his run. He fired the ball as hard and as straight as he could down the wicket towards the bumpy little patch he'd noticed outside off-stump. The ball corkscrewed from his hand. It hit the ground exactly in the middle of the rough, bit and spun back at a wide angle.

Lan was astonished. Almost as astonished as Second Blond, who tried vainly to block the ball's progress with bat and pad. It was useless. He didn't have a chance. The ball ripped past him, the stumps flew back and the bails scattered. The batsman stared in disbelief.

Izram leapt in the air. He rushed down the pitch and threw his arms around Lan. 'Bewdie!' he bellowed. Lan's face split into a grin as the fielders rushed in to congratulate him.

Second Blond was standing frozen. He shifted his gaze from the broken wicket to Drinkwater, who also seemed stunned.

Umpire McGinty raised a finger. Out!

Four down for ninety. Around the oval the spectators had come suddenly alive. Even Larri got up and wagged his tail.

Lan punched the air in triumph. It was a dismissal to set his soul singing.

Stuart Wilson was the next victim, miffed by a brilliant delivery from leg-spinner Lan Nguyen to fall for a duck.

Spinner said later the innings had turned right then and there. One moment King's was on its way to an effortless victory, the next they were shell-shocked by the sheer and unexpected magic of that delivery.

'It sometimes only takes one ball,' Spinner said. ''Course, it has to be a mighty good ball.'

Hiroki's second ball of the sixteenth over took the edge of Jason Crossley's bat and soared towards the sky. There were five people out there ready to take the catch, including Izram at the wicket, but hadn't he, Hiroki, bowled the ball and wasn't he only two metres from the batsman?

Right, Hiroki told himself. I'll have a go at this.

Taking off, he didn't see Sal waiting to catch the ball. He ran into him and knocked him flat. The ball ricocheted off Hiroki's hands and flew away again.

'Jeez, Roki, you couldn't catch a cold,' Sal grumbled, picking himself up.

Right, Hiroki told himself. Messed up that one. Have another go.

At the wicket, Crossley looked amused. Hiroki walked back, his cheeks burning. Lan gave him an encouraging nod. He felt a spurt of optimism and full of purpose. Fingering the little *netsuke* around his neck and murmuring a Buddhist prayer, he bowled a regular medium pacer. Crossley pulled it to mid-wicket. Sal leapt sideways, stuck out his hand and took the catch.

Out!

Nerves obviously played a part as Jason Crossley was out for 15, caught brilliantly in the field by Sal Catano from the bowling of Hiroki Yoshida.

In his office, Mr Drummond heard the roar from the oval. King's had claimed another wicket, he supposed. Then he remembered King's was batting. And there were hardly enough King's supporters at the oval to raise a loud cheer, let alone a roar like that. What was going on?

He looked at his watch. He'd wait for lunch.

Lan looked at the scoreboard. Five down for 125 and five overs remaining. *Matthew Macmillan batted on in a steady partnership with Ben Gunthorpe that had the scoreboard ticking over* ... Andy was finishing his spell, one over left, then it would be his turn. *The pace was building nicely when* ...

Gunthorpe at the striker's end. The two King's batsmen had really knocked Andy to all parts of the ground and he almost walked in, his head low. He bowled a long hop and Gunthorpe smashed it to mid-wicket boundary, an awesome shot that was, as Spinner would say, a four for all money.

David chased it.

Lan, his heart in his mouth, willed him to make it as Andy covered the wicket.

David grabbed the ball just inside the boundary to loud cheers from a class of hysterical Grade 3 students who were sitting nearby. He threw it into Izram's gloves with fantastic accuracy. Izram knocked the bails off and there was Gunthorpe sprawled in the ground just outside the crease.

Run-out!

Six for 135.

With the partnership broken, Macmillan was the mainstay batter with Jeremy Graham offering his captain reasonable support.

Lan knew he had to stop Macmillan getting his fifty. And he had stopped him. He heard Macmillan snick the ball as it flashed past into Izzie's gloves. Iz heard it too because he jumped into the air with a yell. Caught behind! Howzat! Both of them appealed as the spectators yelled and clapped their approval.

Resolutely, Macmillan stood his ground and stared into the distance as if he had no idea what all this juvenile yelling was about.

Drinkwater shook his head. 'Not out,' he called.

Spinner stared straight ahead. At his feet, Larri growled.

Macmillan, expressionless, again took up his stance, ready to face the next ball.

About to open his mouth in protest, Lan caught a warning shake of the head from Spinner. No arguing with the umpire's decision. But he'd snicked the ball. Macmillan knew he'd snicked the ball. Even Larri knew he'd snicked the ball. He should have walked.

Swallowing his outrage, Lan bowled the next ball.

Macmillan, who was lucky to survive a controversial decision by the square leg umpire, batted on to make his 50 ...

Lan and the fielders joined in the applause when the King's captain retired — it was a courtesy that

Spinner insisted on — but Lan felt it hadn't been deserved.

Graham (17) and Toby Burchfield (4) were both not out at the end of overs.

King's six down for 148 runs. It was a good score, although possibly not as good as the visitors had anticipated.

23

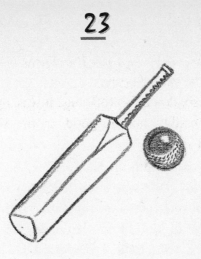

Delicious aromas had been drifting over the pitch all through the final overs as the food stalls on the playground geared up for business and the players' lunch was prepared in the marquee.

The King's First XI were used to traditional cricketing teas of thinly sliced sandwiches and little iced cakes. Mrs Nguyen and her helpers wouldn't have recognised a traditional cricketing tea if it had walked up and bit them.

The players filed into the refreshment tent to be confronted by two long tables groaning with dishes of fragrant and spicy curries, bowls of steamed and fried rice, platters of cold prawn rolls, kebabs, five-spice fried chicken, samosas and spring rolls, steamed lotus buns, satays, tempura, choice pieces of meat and vegetables battered and deep-fried Japanese-style, stacks of tortillas, chappattis, parathas and roti breads, and jugs of lime and orange juice. Never in their lives had they ever sat down to such a glorious spread. With a healthy score on the board and a clear victory in sight, they attacked it with enthusiasm.

Spinner, too, seemed to think the visitors deserved a good feed.

'Take that over to the King's table,' he said to Mrs Hussein, just as she was about to put a huge dish of coconut chicken curry and a platter of warm flaky *puris* in front of him. He sniffed appreciatively at Mrs Chen's *nasi goreng*, took a small serve for himself and then that, too, went across to the other table. 'Get stuck into that, boys!' he called out encouragingly. He refused to let his players touch Mrs Catano's tray of lasagne until the King's team had taken all they wanted, although he heaped a generous portion into Larri's bowl.

'I do congratulate you. This is simply splendid hospitality!' enthused Mr Drinkwater to Mr Drummond.

If the organisation had been left in Mr Drummond's hands they would all have been eating pies, pasties and finger buns in the shelter shed, but the principal accepted the praise with a gracious smile.

At last year's International Food Day Mr Drummond had stood in the playground gnawing at a cold lamb yiros in a paper bag that had leaked garlic sauce down his shirtfront. Now he found himself seated in comfort next to the sports master from King's

College, while charming women heaped all sorts of delicious foods onto his plate. *Have some Tatsuta Age or teriyaki, Mr Drummond ... Have both, Mr Drummond ... Some pandan chicken, some Hokkien Mee for you? ... A few prawn dumplings?*

The principal could have done with less of the recorder band's musical selections (did they have to keep playing 'Amazing Grace'?), but he began to think this cricket business wasn't such a bad idea after all. Definitely a school tradition in the making. Mr Drummond thought he might make a speech. Then he thought he'd better have some of the delicious kofta curry before it all disappeared down the gullets of the King's XI. Good God, they were gluttons! What did that say about the private school system?

Mrs Nguyen brought around one of Lan's favourite dishes, *Ga Nuong Xa Ot,* succulent pieces of chicken grilled with chilli and lemon grass. Lan waited for Spinner to send that over to the King's table, too. He was taking this courtesy thing a little too far, Lan reckoned. It was one thing to applaud good games-manship; quite another to deprive your own players of sustenance.

'I have something special for you, Lan,' his mother said. She handed him a white paper bag.

Curious, he looked inside. A Vegemite sandwich!

Lan was overcome with emotion. In actual fact, he'd take a bowl of *Ga Nuong Xa Ot* over a Vegemite sandwich any day — who wouldn't? — but it made him

feel all choked up to think that his mother had remembered and thought of him and made him something she
knew would please him.

'I see you bowl that big smash ball,' she said
proudly. 'I clap so hard I think my hands drop off.'

From further down the table Mr Burridge heard
her and nodded in affirmation. 'A remarkable delivery!'

'A bloody beauty,' Spinner said. 'A ball to rival the
one Warnie sent down to Gatting in '93, I reckon.'

'I'm glad to see you keeping up with the game,
Clarrie,' Mr Burridge said. 'There's a coaching job at
the club if you want it. You've done wonders with
these lads.' He leant across the table to Lan. 'You come
and see me again in the New Year, young fellow. And
where's that lad who took that stupendous catch at
mid-field?'

'That was my Salvatore!' Mrs Catano exclaimed,
waving her serving spoon proudly in his direction.
Globs of lasagne flew everywhere. A big runny one
landed on Second Blond's head.

The Nips had all done well, Lan thought. But this
wasn't the time to relax. They had a big innings in front
of them. He nibbled at his sandwich. Suddenly it was
all he wanted to eat. It was all he *could* eat. He looked
around the table. The others weren't eating much
either. There was nothing like knowing you were about
to face a Mac attack to put you off your food.

He saw Mrs Chen coming towards them carrying
a large platter of watermelon. Ah, his favourite fruit!

He could really go a slice or two of watermelon. But Spinner jumped up, took the platter from her hands and delivered it to the King's table. Matthew Macmillan immediately reached for a slice.

Lan grabbed what was rest of his Vegemite sandwich. 'You're not thinking of giving them this too, are you?' he grumbled.

'Where's yer sense of hospitality?' Spinner said. 'They're our guests.'

'What about Ma's coconut custard? You're not going to send that over to them?'

'I already have,' Spinner said.

24

Did Steve Waugh feel like this while he waited to bat? Lan wondered. Jittery. Tense. In and out of the toilet. Akram had been so nervous he'd managed to fasten his batting pads together at the knees. When it came his turn to stride to the wicket he'd fallen flat on his face.

'It's different when you get to the crease,' David said. 'Then you sort of become cool and calm.'

But David would be cool and calm in a hurricane, Lan thought. Look at the way he'd hung in there when Big Mac had demoralised them all by clean bowling poor Izzie. 'All those curries and you can't get the runs!' he'd jeered, as Izram left the field.

Lan's heart had sunk. One wicket for four.

But David had stayed in, surviving a few hairy moments but steadily adding runs to the board. He,

Akka and, to everyone's surprise, fourth bat, Andy, took the total to fifty.

It wasn't brilliant batting, however, that kept the Nips at the crease. As the game progressed, the bowlers' pace dropped off and the fielding got progressively worse. The slips missed two easy catches, the out-fielders were caught napping and the wicket-keeper looked as if any moment he might slump over and dislodge the bails without any help from the ball.

How had they lost form so quickly? Lan wondered. Why were they so *slow*?

Spinner caught his eye and winked. And suddenly Lan felt like laughing. The cunning old bugger! So that was the reason for his generous hospitality at lunchtime!

A twenty-course Asian banquet played havoc with King's after-lunch innings. 'The curries knocked us back a bit but personally I blame the watermelon,' said Captain Matthew Macmillan. 'It looked innocent, but it was lethal.'

Lan brightened up. The game might have a different ending after all.

David made his half-century to wild applause from the spectators. Most of the school were on the oval now, even the ones who had little idea of the state of play and needed constant reassurance. 'Who's winning? Are we winning?' they demanded. 'Nobody's winning,' Mr Thistleton kept explaining patiently. 'Nobody's won or lost until the last ball's been bowled.'

But King's weren't intercollegiate champions for nothing and by drinks the score was six for seventy-five.

'Good luck,' Lan said to Phon as he went in to bat. 'Watch out for Wilson's leg-cutter.'

A look of terror came over Phon's face. He had no idea what a leg-cutter was but it sounded fatal. He trudged off, his knees quaking. He faced Wilson with the look of a startled rabbit caught in the headlights just before it is squished to death.

By the time Lan went in to bat the score was seven for eighty-two. They were in with a slight chance, but a chance nonetheless. All he had to do was stay in and make his fifty runs. The headline wrote itself in his head: *Who says Nips can't play cricket! A journey from the depths of despair to the heights of glory ... Today at the NICG, victory was snatched from the jaws of defeat ...*

At the other end Satria gave him a thumbs up and Larri wagged his tail encouragingly. Lan came back to earth. There were plenty of overs to go. Take it easy, he told himself, and play yourself in.

He took a deep breath. His Vegemite sandwich was a distant memory, but the bowler who came trundling down the pitch looked as if most of Mrs Nguyen's coconut custard was still sloshing around in his tummy. He bowled a stock leggie. Lan swung his bat and the ball raced off the middle of the bat past cover point for four.

It was a beautiful drive. The crowd yelled and cheered.

Lan stayed in. His nervousness had vanished. The runs mounted.

Satria was out, caught in the slips for fifteen. Sal came in and was out for ten. King's had regained the upper hand and as their confidence soared anew, so did their contempt. Lan felt his resentment beginning to grow. He disliked the opposition's loud triumphs and the way they screamed and carried on after each dismissal. What was the point of giving an angry stare and a mouthful to a batsman *after* you'd bowled him out?

His anger seemed to fuel his determination. Now he *really* wanted to win. Between balls, his eyes flicked over the ground, taking in the position of the field. The fielders came in closer and he belted a cover drive to wild applause. Spinner nodded in appreciation.

Nine for 125. Lan Nguyen not out for thirty.

Hiroki was their last batsman. Lan could see he was nervous. He'd turned into a good reliable bowler but he was uncoordinated when he was wielding a bat. On the other hand, he was fiercely determined. Lan told him, 'Hang in there, Roki. Just try and keep out the balls that might hit the stumps and go for safe singles. If I can get my fifty we've won.'

They were twenty-three runs behind when Macmillan came back to bowl his final three overs. He gave Lan a stony look and made a big show of re-organising his field. The slips and gullies crowded around in anticipation. The intention was clear: demolish the skipper and it was all over.

Macmillan rubbed the sweat from his brow on the ball then polished it vigorously on his trousers. He gave one of his infamous scowls, raked his hair back, and thundered down the pitch.

It was a scorcher. Lan sensed rather than saw it and he stuck out his bat as it flashed past and into the keeper's gloves. Bummer! He'd snicked it.

Ignoring the umpire, Macmillan raced down the pitch screaming his triumph. The wicket-keeper yelled, his arms in the air. The fielders ran in and pounded their captain on the back.

On the benches, the Nips groaned. A sigh ran around the oval.

Disappointment kept Lan rooted to the wicket. The fate of the match had been in his hands. Between them, he and Hiroki could have got those remaining runs.

Incredibly, however, Drinkwater had not given him out. Perhaps he didn't appreciate the way Big Mac had totally ignored him, Lan thought. Any minute now he'd put up his finger.

But Drinkwater shook his head and kept his hands resolutely clasped behind his back. 'Not out,' he said.

Macmillan, his mouth slack in outrage, threw his arms out in disbelief.

The crowd showed their approval.

But he'd snicked the ball. Lan tucked his bat under his left arm and started to walk off.

'Get back!' Hiroki hissed.

'I didn't give you out, son,' Drinkwater called.

Lan shook his head. 'I snicked it, sir.' That was how Spinner had taught them to play the game. With honour. No sledging. No cheating. And if you snicked the ball, you walked.

Macmillan stared at him. He despises me, Lan thought. Thinks I'm a loser. The spectators, too, were confused. 'What's going on?' they asked each other. But Larri wagged his tail again as he went off and Spinner gave him the nod. 'Well played, mate,' he said quietly. He sounded proud.

That was all Lan needed. He walked off with his head high, writing the final line in his head: *Nguyen's luck ran out when he was caught behind by Crossley after snicking a fast-paced delivery from Macmillan. King's won by 23 runs.*

For a brief moment, Lan felt a pang of regret. Perhaps he should have stayed at the wicket and accepted the umpire's wrong call. They might just have won. They'd been so close to winning. Now it was all over Red Rover. How would the team react? Would they think he'd let them down?

Tomas ran up and threw his arms around him. 'We almost won!' he exclaimed excitedly.

The truth dawned on Lan: *they'd almost won.*

The others ran up. Some of them were disappointed,

he could see. But he met them proudly. 'We almost won!' he said. 'Howzat!'

They grinned at each other. They gave each other high fives. Lan felt a lump growing in his throat. He stared out at the pitch where players and umpires were shaking hands. Larri yapped joyously and Spinner beckoned them all onto the field.

Applause rang in his ears. Mr Burridge shook his hand. 'Well done, son, well played. I haven't enjoyed a game of cricket so much for years.' Then it was Mr Thistleton, patting him on the back. '... proud of you, Lan ... of all you boys ... a fine game played in the right spirit.'

Mr Drinkwater shook his hand firmly and told him he hoped he'd go on playing because the game needed true sportsmen like him. Matthew Macmillan offered his hand and Lan didn't miss the look of shame in his eyes. No, he thought, it's not worth winning if you feel like that afterwards.

In fact, for a team that had won, King's seemed strangely subdued. Refusing the offer of refreshment, they packed up their gear and headed off towards their mini-bus. A group of Grade 4 girls were playing hop-scotch on the edge of the playground and called out as they went past, 'Did you win or did we win?'

Nobody answered.

On the oval, the Nips were surrounded by their parents and families. Mr Hussein thumped everyone on the back in delight. 'Well played, Lan!' *Thump*. 'Bad luck, Izzie, but what about that catch in the first innings, eh?' *Thump*. 'What do you think of our boys, Mr Spinner?' *Thump*.

'They played the game I taught them,' Spinner said. 'Can't ask more than that.'

'I cheered for you even when you weren't winning,' his mother said proudly. 'That's what Australians do in cricket, yes?'

Two small figures in orange shorts and striped tops rushed up and grabbed his legs. And to Lan's astonishment, there was his father. His father never took a day off. 'What about the shop?' Lan blurted out.

His father grinned. 'Bugger the shop! Think I would miss seeing my son play such a match?'

'Bugger the shop!' Tien echoed.

Lan gaped. When had his father learnt that word?

His father grinned at him. 'We are all turning Australian!'

'We won! We won!' carolled Linh, dancing around with Larri in her arms. 'We won, didn't we, Lan?'

He shook his head.

'The game won,' Spinner said, his eyes suspiciously moist. 'But the Nips didn't do too bad either.'

Mr Hussein didn't believe in understatement. 'They were magnificent!' he roared. 'They are heroes!'

Everybody laughed and applauded.

In his office where he had snoozed away most of the afternoon, Mr Drummond was alerted by Mrs Moody that the match on the oval seemed to be over.

He stood up, stretched, and gathered his notes together. As he strode across the playground the King's mini-bus pulled out of the car park. But the principal didn't see it. He was rehearsing his speech.

The home team has lost today ...

He stopped. Had they in fact lost? Yes, they must have. Of course they had lost, a scrappy team like that. Nobody had given them the remotest chance against the district's finest.

How could he soften the blow? What did one say on an occasion like this? He glanced at his notes for inspiration.

But it has been a magnificent game. Both teams have upheld the highest traditions of Australian sports-manship ...

That would do.

Mr Drummond walked on, wondering if there was any of that delicious kofta curry left.